Elizabeth went straight to her locker when she arrived at school on Monday morning. It was bad enough not having Todd to talk to anymore, but to go through the entire weekend without her journal, especially after all that had happened, was almost more than she could stand. "Please let it be there," she whispered as she unlocked the door. But just as she pulled it open, Kris slipped in front of her. He was holding out a single white rose. "What's this?" she asked.

"A peace offering," said Kris. "I want to apologize for the other night. I really went off the deep end, and I'm sorry." He handed her the rose. "Say you'll forgive me."

"If you'll forgive me," Elizabeth said. "I never meant to hurt you."

By the time Kris left her, Elizabeth had almost forgotten what she had been doing when he interrupted her. It wasn't until she reached into the locker for her books that she remembered her journal. But it wasn't on the shelf. *I don't believe this,* she said to herself. *If it's not here, where can it be?* And then she saw it, jammed beneath her sneakers on the locker floor. She picked up the journal and tucked it into her bag. *I really should keep track of where I put this,* she thought. *Or some stranger may get to read the life and times of Elizabeth Wakefield!*

Bantam Books in the Sweet Valley High series
Ask your bookseller for the books you have missed

#1 DOUBLE LOVE
#2 SECRETS
#3 PLAYING WITH FIRE
#4 POWER PLAY
#5 ALL NIGHT LONG
#6 DANGEROUS LOVE
#7 DEAR SISTER
#8 HEARTBREAKER
#9 RACING HEARTS
#10 WRONG KIND OF GIRL
#11 TOO GOOD TO BE TRUE
#12 WHEN LOVE DIES
#13 KIDNAPPED!
#14 DECEPTIONS
#15 PROMISES
#16 RAGS TO RICHES
#17 LOVE LETTERS
#18 HEAD OVER HEELS
#19 SHOWDOWN
#20 CRASH LANDING!
#21 RUNAWAY
#22 TOO MUCH IN LOVE
#23 SAY GOODBYE
#24 MEMORIES
#25 NOWHERE TO RUN
#26 HOSTAGE!
#27 LOVESTRUCK
#28 ALONE IN THE CROWD
#29 BITTER RIVALS
#30 JEALOUS LIES
#31 TAKING SIDES
#32 THE NEW JESSICA
#33 STARTING OVER
#34 FORBIDDEN LOVE
#35 OUT OF CONTROL
#36 LAST CHANCE
#37 RUMORS
#38 LEAVING HOME
#39 SECRET ADMIRER
#40 ON THE EDGE
#41 OUTCAST
#42 CAUGHT IN THE MIDDLE
#43 HARD CHOICES
#44 PRETENSES
#45 FAMILY SECRETS
#46 DECISIONS
#47 TROUBLEMAKER
#48 SLAM BOOK FEVER
#49 PLAYING FOR KEEPS
#50 OUT OF REACH
#51 AGAINST THE ODDS
#52 WHITE LIES
#53 SECOND CHANCE
#54 TWO-BOY WEEKEND
#55 PERFECT SHOT
#56 LOST AT SEA
#57 TEACHER CRUSH
#58 BROKENHEARTED
#59 IN LOVE AGAIN
#60 THAT FATAL NIGHT
#61 BOY TROUBLE
#62 WHO'S WHO?
#63 THE NEW ELIZABETH
#64 THE GHOST OF TRICIA MARTIN
#65 TROUBLE AT HOME
#66 WHO'S TO BLAME?
#67 THE PARENT PLOT
#68 THE LOVE BET
#69 FRIEND AGAINST FRIEND
#70 MS. QUARTERBACK
#71 STARRING JESSICA!
#72 ROCK STAR'S GIRL
#73 REGINA'S LEGACY
#74 THE PERFECT GIRL
#75 AMY'S TRUE LOVE
#76 MISS TEEN SWEET VALLEY
#77 CHEATING TO WIN
#78 THE DATING GAME
#79 THE LONG-LOST BROTHER
#80 THE GIRL THEY BOTH LOVED
#81 ROSA'S LIE
#82 KIDNAPPED BY THE CULT!
#83 STEVEN'S BRIDE
#84 THE STOLEN DIARY

Super Editions:
PERFECT SUMMER
SPECIAL CHRISTMAS
SPRING BREAK
MALIBU SUMMER
WINTER CARNIVAL
SPRING FEVER

Super Thrillers:
DOUBLE JEOPARDY
ON THE RUN
NO PLACE TO HIDE
DEADLY SUMMER

Super Stars:
LILA'S STORY
BRUCE'S STORY
ENID'S STORY
OLIVIA'S STORY

Magna Edition:
THE WAKEFIELDS OF SWEET VALLEY

THE STOLEN DIARY

Written by
Kate William

Created by
FRANCINE PASCAL

BANTAM BOOKS
NEW YORK • TORONTO • LONDON • SYDNEY • AUCKLAND

RL 6, age 12 and up

THE STOLEN DIARY
A Bantam Book / April 1992

Conceived by Francine Pascal

Produced by Daniel Weiss Associates, Inc.
33 West 17th Street
New York, NY 10011

Cover art by James Mathewuse

ISBN 0-553-29230-7

Published simultaneously in the United States and Canada

Bantam Books are published by Bantam Books, a division of Bantam Doubleday Dell Publishing Group, Inc. Its trademark, consisting of the words "Bantam Books" and the portrayal of a rooster, is Registered in U.S. Patent and Trademark Office and in other countries. Marca Registrada. Bantam Books, 666 Fifth Avenue, New York, New York 10103.

PRINTED IN THE UNITED STATES OF AMERICA

OPM 0 9 8 7 6 5 4 3 2 1

To Cici Johansson

One

"What's the matter?" Enid Rollins teased. "You lose your other half?"

Elizabeth Wakefield and her best friend, Enid, were having lunch together in the Sweet Valley High cafeteria. Enid was eating and talking with her usual enthusiasm, but Elizabeth was distracted. Every few minutes she looked up, and her pretty blue-green eyes would scan the busy room, searching for her boyfriend, Todd Wilkins. Normally, Todd ate his lunch with Elizabeth, but this Monday he was nowhere to be seen.

"Oh, don't say that," she pleaded, returning her attention to her friend. "Ever since Steven and Cara nearly eloped, I've been feeling like Todd and I are an old married couple."

Elizabeth smiled, showing the mischievous dimple in her left cheek, but in her heart she knew that she was far from joking. Recently, her older brother, Steven, a student at the nearby state university, had almost given up his chance to go to law school in order to marry his girlfriend, Cara Walker. Cara's mother had accepted a job in London, and Steven and Cara were so upset by the idea of being separated that they had decided to elope. In the end, friends and family had helped convince them that they were too young to make such a commitment, but their predicament had forced Elizabeth and Todd to examine their own relationship more closely.

Elizabeth made a face. "Sixteen and settled!" she said with a laugh.

"Well, it's better than sixteen and suffering," said Enid.

"Enid," Elizabeth asked, immediately becoming serious, "is something wrong?"

"Not really." Enid shrugged. "Well . . . oh, I don't know, Liz. It's just that I've been missing Hugh a lot lately."

Enid had dated handsome Hugh Grayson for some time, and Elizabeth knew how much her friend had liked him. The problem had been that Hugh lived in Big Mesa, not in Sweet Valley. Living in different towns and going to different schools had made it difficult for the couple to spend much time together, and eventually they had agreed to break up.

"I mean, I know we had our problems," Enid continued, "and it isn't easy dating someone who lives miles away, but the truth is that I just haven't liked any of the other boys I've gone out with half as much as Hugh." She pushed away her half-eaten sandwich. "What's a girl to do?" she joked.

Elizabeth leaned toward her. "Well," she said slowly, "a girl *could* tell Hugh exactly how she feels."

Enid stared back in horror. "Oh, I couldn't do that," she said hastily. "I heard that he's been dating someone else lately. What if he rejects me?"

"Don't be ridiculous," said Elizabeth. "First of all, just because you heard rumors doesn't mean that they're true. And, second of all, you know how much Hugh likes you. Even if he *is* involved with someone else, I don't see what you have to lose by being truthful with him."

Enid groaned. "You mean honesty is the best policy, right?"

"Exactly."

Enid shook her head. "I don't know, Liz. It was really hard for me when Hugh and I broke up. I know it was mutual and for the best and everything, but I never really believed we'd stop seeing each other. I think I honestly believed that he'd drive up to my house one day, take me into his arms, and tell me I was the only girl for him."

"You mean like a knight on a white horse," Elizabeth said with a grin.

"More like a knight in a red Volkswagen. Anyway, the point is that he didn't."

"But that was a while ago," Elizabeth argued. "Now he's had plenty of time to realize how much he misses you."

"Or how much he doesn't miss me." Enid shook her curly reddish-brown hair. "Really, Liz, I couldn't go through the pain and humiliation again." She shuddered. "All those nights I sat by the telephone thinking he was going to call. No,

I'd rather suffer in silence than risk having Hugh turn me down flat." She helped herself to one of Elizabeth's cookies. "Why does love have to be so difficult?" she asked with a sigh.

Elizabeth's eyes began to twinkle. "You know what I think? I think we need a little advice from someone who's an expert in this sort of thing."

Enid turned pale and dropped the cookie in terror. "You're sworn to secrecy, Elizabeth Wakefield!" she gasped. "If anyone ever found out about this . . . if *Hugh* ever found out—"

"Enid, get a grip on yourself. I'm not going to tell anyone!" Elizabeth laughed. "All I meant was that we should try to imagine what Jessica would do if she were in this situation. You know, if she wanted to let a boy know that she liked him without actually coming out and saying anything."

Enid retrieved her cookie. "You mean we have to be clever and subtle."

"I mean we have to be clever and *sneaky*." Elizabeth grinned conspiratorially.

Enid glanced at her watch. "Well, we'll have to be sneaky later," she said, pushing back her chair and getting to her feet. "Look at the time! Lunch period's almost over!"

Elizabeth stood up, too. "I wonder where Todd could be," she mused, giving one more look around the cafeteria. "It's not like him to miss a meal."

Enid scooped up her books. "Something probably came up," she said lightly. "You know what Mondays are like."

* * *

Elizabeth looked at her watch for the third time that minute and drummed her fingers on the steering wheel. "Where is she?" she asked the rearview mirror.

Jessica Wakefield was late. Again. Although Jessica looked exactly like her twin sister, from her sun-streaked blond hair and sparkling blue-green eyes to her perfect size-six figure and contagious smile, in reality she couldn't have been more different from Elizabeth than if she had been born to completely different parents. Not only was Jessica frivolous, flirtatious, and fun-loving while Elizabeth was serious, steadfast, and studious, she was also always late.

Just then Elizabeth spotted her twin across the lawn. Jessica was hurrying toward the twins' red Fiat Spider with a big smile on her face, her schoolbooks held against her chest, and her hair blowing in the breeze.

"I hope you haven't been waiting long," she said as she slid into the seat beside Elizabeth. "I got held up."

Elizabeth could never stay angry with Jessica for long, and this afternoon was no exception. An impish smile lit up her face. "Not by a boy, I hope," she teased.

Jessica laughed. "Just because I'm going out with Sam doesn't mean I can't talk to other boys. After all, I don't want to lose my touch, you know. What happens if Sam and I break up someday? I've heard of people who go for weeks without another date." She shivered in mock horror.

Elizabeth started the engine. The Fiat wheezed for a second or two, and then the engine turned over and they started to move. "I'm sure there's no danger of you losing your touch. In fact," she went on, remembering her lunchtime conversation with Enid, "I was wondering if you could give me some tips on how to get a boy to ask you out."

Jessica turned to her sister, her eyes wide with amazement. *"You?"* Jessica hooted. "What happened to Todd? Don't tell me he's been kidnapped by aliens!"

"No." Elizabeth laughed. "He's still on this planet. I was just thinking about doing an article for *The Oracle*. You know, a funny look at how girls get boys interested in them, and I thought you might be able to help me out." Elizabeth didn't want to lie to her twin, but she couldn't betray Enid's trust, either. *Perhaps I really will write an article on this,* Elizabeth thought. Elizabeth often wrote articles for the school paper as well as her weekly column, "Eyes and Ears."

Jessica groaned dramatically. "I can't believe we share the same genes," she said. "What I know about boys would fill a book, but what you know wouldn't fill a postcard." She shook her shining hair. "You and Todd have been together so long, I bet neither of you remembers what a real date is like."

Elizabeth laughed. "OK, Jess, since I know *nothing* about boys or dating, let's say there's a boy you like who goes to a different school. How would you get him to notice you?"

Jessica turned to her sister, her eyes sparkling mischievously. "What are his hobbies, what are his interests, and where does he hang out?"

* * *

After dinner that evening, Elizabeth met Todd in the library, as they had arranged the day before. Both of them were busy researching different school projects, so she didn't think anything of the fact that he seemed rather distant and quiet. It wasn't until they were getting ready to leave that he finally spoke to her. "Do you have your car, or would you like a lift home?" he asked.

Elizabeth smiled. "Jessica's taken the Fiat to Lila's," she said, "so if you don't mind . . ."

Todd shrugged. "No, I don't mind."

"Well, you don't have to sound so enthusiastic," Elizabeth kidded him as they walked to his car. "I'm sure I could find somebody else to drive me home if I'm taking you out of your way."

She waited for his usual lopsided grin, but instead Todd just mumbled something about feeling tired.

Elizabeth climbed into the BMW. "No wonder you're tired," she said, buckling her seatbelt. "You've been working nonstop all day. Where were you at lunch?"

Todd got into the driver's seat. "Lunch?" he said vaguely.

Elizabeth looked at him quizzically. "Yes," she said, "lunch. You remember lunch, Todd. It's that meal in the middle of the day. The one you usually spend with me?"

"Oh, right, lunch." He started the engine. "I guess I forgot to tell you. I'd promised to give someone some help with their math homework today."

"Well, I'm glad you're such a good friend," she teased, "but I missed you. My cheese sandwich just doesn't taste the same when you're not there."

The car jumped forward so abruptly that the back of Elizabeth's head bounced against the headrest. But instead of asking her if she was all right, Todd turned on her. "Come on, Liz," he said sharply, "you can eat lunch without me for one day, can't you?"

Elizabeth stared at him in surprise. "Of course I can," she replied, feeling oddly defensive. "I only meant that we usually eat lunch together, that's all."

"*Usually* isn't the same as *must*," Todd said, concentrating on the road ahead. "If I want to do something else once in a while, I can. It's not like you own me or anything, you know. We may go out together, but I'm still a free agent."

Elizabeth couldn't believe what she was hearing. She folded her arms across her chest and stared out the window. This wasn't like Todd at all. Elizabeth was never overly possessive, and he knew it.

The car came to a sudden stop in front of the Wakefields' home.

Elizabeth glanced around in surprise. Todd was leaning back in the driver's seat, his eyes on some distant point down the road. "Todd," said Elizabeth, somehow managing to control the anger she was beginning to feel, "I really don't understand what's going on."

"Nothing's going on, Elizabeth," Todd replied, not turning to look at her. "I just don't think I have to ask your permission if I feel like doing something without you."

Elizabeth unsnapped her seatbelt with a clang. "Look, Todd," she said, straining to stay calm, "I certainly don't want you to feel that you need my permission for anything. I'm your girlfriend, not your mother." She gathered her books in her arms. "If you're feeling so smothered by me, maybe we shouldn't see quite so much of each other for a while." She froze with her hand on the door handle, waiting for him to say, *Of course I don't want to see less of you, Liz.*

Todd cleared his throat. "Maybe you're right," he said, his voice tight. "Maybe we need a little breather from each other."

Too shocked to trust herself to answer, Elizabeth clamped her mouth shut and stared fixedly at the clock on the dashboard.

"Not just for me," Todd went on quickly. "I mean, ever since Justin Silver, I've had the feeling I was cramping your style."

Justin Silver? Cramping my style? The blue numerals of the clock began to swim before Elizabeth's eyes as a hundred different thoughts raced through her head. Justin Silver had been their bowling coach. He had had a crush on Elizabeth, but though she had been attracted to him, she had stopped short of encouraging him because of her relationship with Todd. *Maybe I should have gone out with him,* she thought, dazed. But it was too late. Justin Silver was dating someone else by then. She had turned a great-looking boy down flat, and for what? For someone who all of a sudden didn't want to go out with her anymore!

Elizabeth was vaguely aware that Todd was still talking. "Don't tell me you weren't attracted to him," Todd was saying. "I'll bet you're sorry now that you didn't go out with him."

Elizabeth's head was reeling. She stared at him silently. Finally, she found her voice. "Maybe I am," she managed to say.

"You see?" said Todd.

A solitary tear slid down Elizabeth's cheek.

Todd touched her shoulder. His voice became more gentle. "Look, Liz," he said, "you know I don't really want to break up with you. It's just that . . . I don't know, we're still so young. I think we both need a little more freedom. You know, just to find out who we are. Maybe even . . . you know . . . start seeing other people."

She turned away. She couldn't look at him anymore. If she looked at him, she really would start to cry. "Other people?" she whispered.

"I'm not saying absolutely," he added quickly. "I'm just saying I'm sure we'd both like the option."

Elizabeth's whisper was like a shadow of her normal voice. "Oh, right," she said. "The option."

"But of course we'll still be friends," Todd continued. "Nothing's going to change that."

What was the point of arguing? What could she say? Todd was right. They were young. Even *she* was afraid that they had become too settled. And anyway, it was obvious that Todd's mind was made up.

With a monumental effort, Elizabeth pushed the car door open. "Of course," she said, her voice sounding flat and loud in the quiet of the night. "Of course we'll still be friends."

Elizabeth had been writing in her journal for twenty minutes, and was beginning to feel better. Talking to herself in her journal always helped. It was the one place where she never had to worry about hurting someone else's feelings or being misunderstood. Writing down exactly what she thought and how she felt helped to put things in perspective. She had written about everything that had happened that evening—everything Todd had said and everything that was going through her head—and the whole horrible night was beginning to make some sense. She could see now that it was not the end of the world. It was a change, but change wasn't necessarily a bad thing. Change could be a good thing, too. And if she was really honest with herself, Todd's feelings were no different from what her own had been lately. Hadn't she joked to Enid just that afternoon that she was "sixteen and settled"? Hadn't there been moments when she *had* wished that she had gone out with Justin Silver? Didn't it upset her every time Jessica suggested that Elizabeth and Todd were boring and dull?

Suddenly, the door to Elizabeth's room burst open.

"I don't believe it!" Jessica fumed, throwing her bag and jacket on the floor and herself down on the bed beside her sister. "I really don't believe it! This is the second time this week!" She turned to her twin. "I can't live like this!" she wailed.

Elizabeth, pen poised and her mind still on her own problems, stared back at her.

Encouraged by what she took to be her sister's interest, Jessica went on. "There I was," she said, "driving along, minding my own business, and what happens? I come to a red light. Being a good driver, of course, I stop at the light. And then, the light changes, but the car won't move. It just makes this funny noise and stops dead. There I am, stalled at a green light, with all these cars behind me honking their horns." She flopped back with an enormous sigh. "Thank goodness there was this cute boy in a Corvette who got me started again. But you can't always count on that. Last time it was a middle-aged woman in a Ford."

"Well," said Elizabeth.

"Well?" Jessica repeated. "Is that all you can say? *Well?*" She propped herself on one elbow and turned to her sister. "Liz," said Jessica, studying her closely, "is something wrong? You look like you've been crying. Has something happened between you and Todd?"

Elizabeth sighed. Jessica was uncanny. Elizabeth had been hoping to keep the news about her and Todd a secret from her twin for at least another day or two, but she could see that there was no way she would be able to. "Sort of," she answered.

Jessica's eyes bored into hers. "Sort of?" she prompted. "Sort of what?"

"Well, we've sort of decided on a . . . a trial separation."

Jessica seemed stunned into silence.

"It's completely mutual," explained Elizabeth

hastily. "We just feel that, you know, maybe we spend too much time together."

"A trial separation?" said Jessica, recovering. A thoughtful look replaced the stunned one. "Whose idea was this trial separation?"

"It was mutual," Elizabeth repeated. "We both thought it would be a good idea."

"Oh, sure," said Jessica, nodding slowly. "Mutual." She frowned, chewing on her bottom lip, a sure sign that she was thinking. "Todd's not interested in somebody else, is he?" she finally asked.

Elizabeth bristled. "Of course not," she snapped. "I mean, we did talk about maybe, uh, eventually seeing other people, but there isn't anyone now." She shut her journal and stuck it under her pillow. "We just felt we need a break from each other, that's all."

"Oh, sure," Jessica said. She sat up, and instantly the thoughtful expression was gone and she was filled with her usual bubbling enthusiasm. "Well, if you ask me, this is probably the best thing that could have happened," she decided. "It'll give you a chance to make some new friends, do some new things." She bounced off the bed and scooped up her things. "Don't you worry," she assured her sister, "because I'm going to make sure that you have so much to do that you won't even notice Todd isn't around."

Elizabeth watched her sister disappear into the bathroom that connected their rooms. She sighed. *I hope Jessica can make me forget that Todd isn't around,* she thought, *but I doubt it.*

Two

"I don't believe it!" Jessica exclaimed as Elizabeth brought the Fiat to a stop in the school parking lot the next morning. "We made it! We actually managed to get here without breaking down!"

"Jessica, please," begged Elizabeth. "If I hear one more word about the car . . ."

Jessica climbed out of the passenger side, banging the door behind her. "Do you think Mom got the hint?" she asked as they started toward the school.

Elizabeth rolled her eyes. "Unless she's suddenly become deaf she did," she said, laughing. "You didn't talk about anything else all through breakfast."

Jessica's expression became thoughtful. "Do you think I should be a little more subtle?" she asked. "I don't want to put too much pressure on her right at the start."

Elizabeth lowered her voice as they neared the

school. "I'll tell you one thing you should be subtle about," she warned, "and that's me and Todd. I don't want you to say anything to Lila Fowler or Caroline Pearce. You know what gossips they are."

Jessica turned to her, the picture of surprise. "I'm shocked!" she cried. "You know how discreet and tactful I can be."

"I know," said Elizabeth, "but I don't often see it. Look how you blabbed about Steven and Cara's elopement!"

"OK, so I told a few friends. I *didn't*, however, tell Mom and Dad. Not until the last minute, anyway." Jessica put two fingers to her mouth. "But look. These lips are sealed," she promised. "You can count on me."

"I don't believe it!" Enid gasped. "You and Todd broke up?"

Elizabeth shook her head. And she had been worried about Jessica and her big mouth! "Enid," she hissed, "keep your voice down, will you? I don't want the whole school to know. Besides, we didn't *break up*. It's just a trial separation."

"Of course it's just temporary," Enid agreed slowly.

"Exactly," said Elizabeth. "And I'm sure it's for the best. I mean, I was pretty upset when he—when we first decided, but now that I've had time to think about it, I can see that it makes a lot of sense. Even the closest couples have to take a break from each other once in a while."

Enid nodded. "Oh, sure. It's like taking separate vacations."

Elizabeth nodded. "Separate vacations describes it perfectly."

Enid leaned against her locker. "You and Todd have such a balanced, mature relationship." She sighed. "I bet if Hugh and I had been more like you two, we'd still be together."

"Or taking separate vacations," said Elizabeth with a grin.

Elizabeth had prepared herself to behave normally when she saw Todd at school. After all, they were still friends. They just were no longer the sort of friends who engaged in long goodbye kisses.

Every time Elizabeth turned a corner that morning she expected to see Todd. And every time she turned a corner she repeated to herself, *Just act normally. Just carry on as though nothing has happened.* But it was lunchtime already, and she hadn't had a chance to act as though nothing had happened. Todd was nowhere to be seen. *He can't be avoiding me, can he?* Elizabeth asked herself as she hurried to the cafeteria. *Don't be silly!* she thought. *Of course he's not avoiding you. He'll be at lunch. You'll see.*

But Todd wasn't at lunch. Elizabeth stood in the doorway of the cafeteria, trying not to look as though she was looking for him, her eyes scanning the noisy crowd. Aaron Dallas . . . Scott Trost . . . Ken Matthews . . . Bruce Patman . . . Andy Jenkins . . . Winston Egbert . . . every boy in the entire world was eating in the school lunchroom that day—every boy with the exception of one. *That's it,* she announced silently. *From now on you will not even think about Todd Wilkins. You will get your mind on something completely different.*

"So what else did Jessica say?" Enid asked eagerly.

Elizabeth had to smile. She hadn't seen Enid this excited in some time. She had decided while she was waiting on the lunch line that the perfect something-completely-different-to-think-about was solving the problem of how to get Enid and Hugh Grayson back together again. Her separation from Todd had been such a shock that she had temporarily forgotten about her earlier conversation with Jessica. But now she had remembered it, and was recounting it for her friend.

Elizabeth made a face. "You wouldn't believe some of the schemes Jessica came up with for catching the attention of cute boys," she said. "Jessica is to romance what Einstein was to physics."

"But what about me?" asked Enid. "What advice applies to me?"

Elizabeth bit into her apple with a thoughtful expression on her pretty face. "Jessica says, 'The first rule for getting a boy interested in you is to make sure he remembers you're alive.' "

Enid ripped open her bag of potato chips so violently that they spilled all over the table. "And how am I going to do that?" she demanded. "We don't go to the same school. We don't hang out at the same places. The only reason he ever came to Sweet Valley was to see me."

"Enid," said Elizabeth patiently, "what would Jessica Wakefield do in this situation?"

Enid thought for half a second. "She'd go to Big Mesa."

"Exactly," said Elizabeth. "And that's what *we're* going to do."

Jessica, having her lunch with Lila Fowler, Amy Sutton, and Caroline Pearce, ate another mouthful of pasta salad and wondered how long her luck would hold. They had been at lunch for over fifteen minutes, and so far the conversation had been all about the upcoming dance, whether or not it should have a special theme, and what colors should never be worn at night. Not one word about Elizabeth and Todd. Jessica's eyes went from Lila to Amy and came to rest on Caroline. Caroline Pearce was the fastest and most efficient means of communication in all of Sweet Valley. Jessica would have liked to believe that the reason no one had mentioned her sister yet was because none of them had heard anything. But she knew that was unrealistic. Caroline often knew what was happening before the people involved did.

And then she saw Caroline and Lila exchange a quick glance. *Here it comes,* she thought to herself. *Caroline's about to change the topic.*

As though reading her mind, Caroline turned to Jessica with a big smile. "I must say, you've been very quiet about what's going on between your sister and Todd."

Jessica looked up, her face blank. "Oh, come on, Caroline," she said dismissively. "You know as well as I do that there's never *anything* going on between Elizabeth and Todd."

Lila raised one perfectly shaped eyebrow. "Oh no?" she asked. "That's not what I heard."

Caroline popped a single grape into her mouth. "And it's certainly not what I heard."

Amy looked from one to the other. "Hey," she broke in, "have I missed something?"

"No," Jessica said firmly.

"You remember that girl we saw on the beach playing volleyball with Todd?" Lila asked Amy.

Amy frowned.

"Skimpy black bikini, dark hair, really nice eyes?"

Amy stopped frowning. "Peggy!" she exclaimed. "Peggy Abbot! She was at Cara's going-away party, too." Amy looked from Lila to Caroline. "You mean . . ."

Caroline nodded. "Exactly. Todd and Elizabeth have split up, and Peggy Abbot is the reason." She broke the surface of another grape with her small white teeth. "Apparently Todd's tired of blondes."

Jessica watched her, amazed at how annoying the way a person ate a grape could be.

"Wow," breathed Amy. "Liz must be really upset."

Lila snorted. "Knowing Liz, she'll probably write an article about it for the paper. 'How to Break Off a Relationship in a Civilized Manner.' "

Jessica pretended to concentrate on her salad. Naturally, she had had her suspicions about Todd's reasons for wanting a trial separation, but she had pushed them aside because Elizabeth had insisted that the decision was mutual and had seemed so convinced that there wasn't another girl involved. Jessica frowned at her lunch. She should know better than to listen to Elizabeth. Elizabeth was so honest and straightforward that she thought everyone else was, too. Jessica gave herself a mental kick. What a dope she had been! Hadn't she seen Todd and Peggy at Cara's party? And hadn't she seen them together at the beach that day? Just because she thought of Todd in much the same way as she thought of her father—solid, dependable, and as dull as a documentary on sea turtles—didn't mean that other girls saw him that way.

"The way I hear it," Caroline continued, "is that this Peggy person has been after Todd for quite some time. She's always following him around." She pushed a strand of hair from her eyes. "She even got him to give her some *special* tutoring in math."

Caroline's laugh is even more annoying than her grape eating, Jessica thought. She looked up, her eyes flashing. "Don't be ridiculous," she snapped. "It's true that Elizabeth and Todd have agreed to cool things off a little, but I know for a fact that he isn't interested in anyone else."

"It isn't ridiculous," put in Lila. "One of the girls in my gym class knows Peggy's best friend, and she says that Peggy's had a crush on Todd for months."

"Just because *she* has a crush on *him* doesn't mean that *he's* interested in *her*," reasoned Jessica.

Caroline smiled. "Oh, really? Then maybe you'd like to tell me who Todd's been having lunch with the last two days."

In spite of herself, Jessica's eyes started moving around the cafeteria.

"Oh, not here," purred Caroline. "In the math room. He's *supposed* to be helping her get ready for her algebra test."

"I'll bet she's good at *division.*" Lila giggled.

"This is really serious," protested Amy. But her voice trailed off into giggles, too.

Jessica scowled. Actually, all of her friends had annoying laughs. Annoying laughs, annoying eating habits, and petty minds. "It was Elizabeth's decision to ease off with Todd," she said stiffly. "If Todd is spending time with Peggy, then it's completely on the rebound."

Lila pulled out her compact to see what damage eating a sandwich had done to her makeup. "Oh, don't be so defensive," she scolded Jessica. "What's the big deal?" She smoothed out her eyebrows. "It might do Elizabeth some good to date someone else for a change." Something very close to a smirk flickered across her lips. "If she can find somebody dull enough, that is."

Jessica got to her feet. "You don't have to worry about my sister," she said coldly, gathering her things together. "If she wants to start seeing other boys, all she has to do is snap her fingers."

"Well, she'd better snap them pretty loudly." Lila laughed. "Considering her taste in men, any boy she'd be interested in will probably be asleep!"

There was no two ways about it, Jessica decided that evening. Elizabeth was avoiding her. She had caught up with her twin after lunch and told her that she had to talk to her about something important, but Elizabeth had put her off. "I'll talk to you when I get home this afternoon," she had promised.

Jessica had waited all afternoon for Elizabeth to come home. It wasn't that she wanted to spread Caroline's gossip, but she did feel Elizabeth had a right to know what everyone was saying.

Elizabeth had finally turned up after the rest of the family had already started to eat. "I'm sorry I'm late," she had apologized, not catching Jessica's eye. "I was held up in a meeting of *The Oracle* staff." She had laughed. "I'm just so busy, I don't know where the time goes!"

She couldn't talk to Jessica after dinner either, because she had had to rush off to the library. "It's this English paper," she had explained. "I really have to finish it this week."

"Liz, please," Jessica had pleaded. "There's something I have to talk to you about."

Elizabeth had pushed past her. "Not now, Jess. When I get home."

Finally Jessica heard the front door open. Elizabeth—at long last—was home. Jessica heard her come in and go straight to her room. *Right,* Jessica said to herself. *Now's the time, before she decides she has another term paper or something that she has to write tonight.*

Jessica went through the bathroom that connected the twins' rooms and stuck her head into her sister's room. "Hi!" she said brightly.

Elizabeth, her head bent over a textbook, didn't look up. "Hi," she said.

Jessica came into the room. "Got a minute?"

Elizabeth sighed. "I don't suppose this could wait till the morning, could it? I've got so much homework, and—"

"Elizabeth," Jessica blurted out, "I think you should know that Todd's seeing someone else."

Elizabeth laughed.

"Liz," said Jessica. "Did you hear me? Todd is seeing someone else."

Elizabeth leaned back in her chair and looked at her. "Jessica," she said, crossing her arms, "Todd and I only decided on this separation yesterday. He can't be seeing someone else."

"I have it on good authority."

Elizabeth's eyes narrowed. "Where did you hear it?" she demanded. "Let me guess," she went on, not giving Jessica an opportunity to answer. "Not from Caroline and Lila, by any chance?"

"Well, as a matter of fact—"

"Really, Jessica," said Elizabeth dismissively. "When are you going to learn? I wouldn't believe anything either of them told me. They'd spread rumors about Santa and Mrs. Claus if they thought they could get away with it."

Jessica didn't know what to do. On one hand, she didn't want Elizabeth to find out about Todd from someone else. On the other hand, she didn't want to push too hard. If Elizabeth didn't want to listen, maybe she shouldn't force her to. Her instincts told her that her sister's bright smile and cheery exterior were probably hiding a lot of confusion and pain. She forced herself to smile. "Well, I know they can get a little carried away sometimes," she said lightly. "It was just that Caroline heard that Todd was hanging out with a girl named Peggy. You know, the one we saw at the beach that time?"

"Caroline's exaggerating, as usual," said Elizabeth. She turned back to her book. "Todd has a lot of friends, Jess. It's only natural that he should spend time with them, and this Patty—"

"Peggy," Jessica corrected.

"—this Peggy is obviously one of them."

Jessica stared at the smooth, golden top of her sister's head for a few seconds. She had tried, she told herself. What more could she do? It was time to change tactics. "You're right," she agreed. "I'm sure that's all it is." She leaned on the back of her sister's chair. "How about doing some hanging out of your own?" she asked casually. "A bunch of us are going to see a movie Thursday night. Why don't you come along?"

Elizabeth looked up. "I'd really like to, Jess," she said, "but there's *The Oracle,* and this English paper, and I've got a test coming up."

"I know how busy you are," said Jessica. "I just thought that, you know, if you were free . . ."

"If I can make it, I'd love to come." Elizabeth smiled. "OK?"

"Sure." Jessica smiled back. "That's great." But inside she was determined not to let her sister crawl into her shell. *I know you, Elizabeth Wakefield,* she told her silently. *You use work as a substitute for life. But this time I'm not going to let it happen!*

Three

Jessica came down to breakfast on Thursday morning just in time to hear her mother say to Elizabeth, "Well, things certainly must be very hectic at school. It's been days since we've seen anything of Todd."

Jessica, standing just outside the kitchen, had to suppress a smile. Mrs. Wakefield never missed a trick. Just two days without seeing Todd's BMW in the driveway or his lean body on one of the kitchen chairs, and already she knew something was up.

Elizabeth, who was eating her cereal and going over her article for the paper at the same time, looked up with a puzzled expression. "What was that?" she asked.

"I said, we haven't seen Todd around for a little while," her mother repeated.

Under her mother's steady gaze, Elizabeth blushed. Jessica groaned silently. Elizabeth had asked her not to say anything to their parents about the situation with Todd because she didn't want to upset them for nothing.

"Well, that's a little unusual, isn't it?" Mrs. Wakefield persisted. "He usually stops by or calls at least once a day."

"Oh, well, you know," Elizabeth stammered, "we've both got so much to do. . . ."

Jessica sighed. As usual, she was going to have to rescue her twin.

"Good morning!" she cried as she breezed into the kitchen. She threw her books on the table, and went over and put her arms around her mother. "Mom," she coaxed, "I want you to do me one tiny little favor."

"Jessica," began Mrs. Wakefield, "your sister and I were in the middle of a conversation."

Out of the corner of her eye, Jessica could see her sister give her a grateful look.

"Two minutes, Mom," she promised. "Two incredibly insignificant minutes in your life. Please."

Mrs. Wakefield looked wary. "What do you want me to do?"

"Just listen to the Fiat."

Mrs. Wakefield shook herself free of her daughter's embrace. "Jessica," she said firmly, "your father told you—"

"Mom, all I'm asking is that you listen. Is that too much to ask? Just listen. And after you've listened, if you still think that it doesn't sound like there are rocks in the engine, then I won't say another word about it as long as I live."

"As long as you live?" asked Mrs. Wakefield.

Jessica looked up at the ceiling. "Well, at least for a day or two," she amended.

"Do you think I should change?" Enid asked.

She and Elizabeth were going over their plans for that afternoon. Right after school, they were driving out to Moon Beach to initiate phase one of Operation Hugh Grayson. Enid, of course, was familiar with Hugh's usual haunts. He was an avid cyclist and did a lot of riding along the coast road. If they didn't see him riding along the road, and if he was nowhere to be found along the beach or at the Moon Beach Café, where a lot of the local teenagers hung out, then they would drive into Big Mesa itself. Enid had heard that Hugh had a part-time job somewhere in town.

"Change?" Elizabeth grinned. "Change into what?"

"Somebody else," joked Enid. "Somebody devastatingly gorgeous who will make Hugh fall madly in love with her at first sight."

"Well, that's one idea that hadn't occurred to me," Elizabeth answered. "But there's a drawback, you know. He'll never realize you want to get back together with him if you show up as someone else."

Enid shrugged. "No, seriously," she said, "do you think I should get out of my school clothes before we go? If we do run into Hugh, I don't want to look awful."

Elizabeth patted her friend's hand. "Don't worry," she said, "you never look awful. And you look absolutely terrific today. That outfit's really great."

"It should be." Enid laughed. "I spent hours last night picking something out, and then I still changed three times this morning."

"I'm glad you decided on the casual look. We certainly wouldn't want Hugh to think you were after him or anything!"

"Enid," Elizabeth said as they passed the sign that welcomed them to Big Mesa, "will you stop fussing? You look great."

"I knew I should have gotten my hair cut last week," Enid moaned. "It looks like a bad wig."

"It does not," said Elizabeth firmly. "It looks great. *You* look great."

"I look like an owl. It's my nose. I never noticed it before, but my nose definitely makes me look like an owl." Enid cast one last baleful glance at herself before tossing her mirror back into her bag.

Elizabeth shook her head, and her sun-streaked blond hair shimmered. "Where to first?" she asked. "Should we just ride along the coast for a while?"

"Ride along the coast? If he's out on his bike, Liz, he could be thirty miles north or south of here. I have to be home by six."

"OK, so you think we should just go straight to Moon Beach?" Without waiting for a reply, Elizabeth took the turnoff for the café.

Enid leaned her head against the car window. "He won't be there," she said gloomily. "This whole idea was crazy. What are the chances that we're going to be at the right place at the right time and run into Hugh?"

Elizabeth pulled into the parking lot of the Moon Beach Café and stopped the Fiat near the entrance. "Are we betting?" she asked with a grin.

"What?"

Elizabeth nodded through the windshield. Enid followed her eyes. There, just locking his bike into the rack, was Hugh Grayson. Enid caught her breath. "I don't believe it!" she whispered. "Look at him. He looks wonderful."

"It must be fate." Elizabeth gave Enid a little shove. "Come on," she urged her, "let's get out of the car."

Enid held on to her seatbelt. "I don't think I can go through with this, Liz," she hissed. "I'm not like Jessica. I don't have any real talent for this sort of thing."

Leaning across her, Elizabeth opened the passenger door. "Out," she ordered.

"I think I've changed my mind," said Enid. "What's that old saying? Let sleeping dogs lie?"

"The old saying I'm thinking of is: Strike while the iron is hot," said Elizabeth. "Out."

"Elizabeth . . ."

"Enid!"

"Enid! Elizabeth!"

Both girls looked up. Hugh Grayson was standing in front of the car, waving at them.

"I don't believe it!" he said. He seemed to be directing his words to Elizabeth, but his eyes kept darting to Enid. "What are you two doing here?"

Enid turned to Elizabeth.

"The car's been acting up lately," Elizabeth answered smoothly, "so we thought we'd take it for a good run."

"Well, what do you know," Hugh said. His smile was becoming a little desperate as he looked directly at Enid. "This is the last place I ever expected to run into you two."

Enid looked back at him. "Yeah . . . well . . . us, too," she mumbled.

Except for the sounds of squawking gulls and pounding surf, Moon Beach was silent. Elizabeth cleared her throat. "We were just going to get a soda," she said brightly. "Why don't you join us, Hugh?"

Hugh looked nervously at Enid. "Well, I don't know if . . ."

Elizabeth gave her friend a nudge.

"Oh, come on," Enid said. "I'll bet you're thirsty if you've been riding all afternoon."

"OK." Hugh laughed. "If you insist."

"Well," said Elizabeth as the Fiat made its way back to Sweet Valley, "you two certainly had a lot to say to each other."

Enid hugged herself. "I'd forgotten how much I like his company," she confessed. "When we were going out, we could talk for hours and hours, about nothing and everything."

Elizabeth was about to say that it was exactly the same with her and Todd when she suddenly remembered that they *weren't* together anymore. She pushed the thought from her mind. "I have a hunch he misses you as much as you miss him," she said instead. "Now all you have to do is think of some reason to call him."

"Me?" Enid gasped. "Call *him?*"

Elizabeth's eyes were sparkling. "Enid," she reminded her, "it isn't as though you don't know this boy. You went out with him!"

"That was a long time ago," Enid said. "I wouldn't know what to say to him now. I mean, I can't just phone him and say, 'Hey, Hugh, now that we've had a soda together, why don't we start dating again?' "

"Of course not. Jessica would think of some brilliant excuse for calling him up."

"Uh-huh." Enid nodded. "And what would it be?"

Elizabeth tapped the steering wheel. "I've got it! You could tell him that you think you lost an earring in the café, and you could ask him to ask about it the next time he's there."

Enid shook her head. "I couldn't. I was nervous enough just now. What if he figures out what I'm doing?"

"He probably won't." Elizabeth assured her as they turned onto the main street of Sweet Valley. "Jessica says that boys don't think like that. And anyway, if he does, he'll be flattered."

"Hey, look!" Enid suddenly shouted. "There's Todd's car!"

Elizabeth came to a stop at the intersection and looked over. It *was* Todd's car. And getting into it were Todd and a pretty dark-haired girl she vaguely recognized from school. They were both laughing.

Enid whistled. "What's *she* doing with Todd?'

Elizabeth managed to keep her voice casual "Oh, she's probably in one of his classes or some thing. I bet he's just giving her a lift home."

But Enid was shaking her head. "She can't b in any of his classes. I'm sure she's a sophomore I wish I could remember her name."

Elizabeth accelerated so suddenly that Enic bounced back against her seat with a cry o surprise.

"It's Peggy," said Elizabeth, adding to herself *Peggy from the beach.*

After she dropped Enid off, Elizabeth drove i circles for a while. She didn't want to go straigh home. She needed some time to get her thought together. Seeing Todd with another girl had upse her. There was no point in pretending that i hadn't. It was the surprise more than anythin else. Of course, she reminded herself, the mer fact that they were getting into his car together smiling like idiots, didn't mean that there wa anything between them.

Elizabeth turned left again. "Who am I kid ding?" she wondered out loud. "That's the gir Jessica was trying to warn me about."

All right, so maybe there was more to Carolin and Lila's gossip than she had wanted to believe Maybe seeing Peggy with Todd explained why Todd was never around at lunchtime anymore Maybe it explained why he thought it was bes for them to have a trial separation.

Tired of driving up and down the same roads, Elizabeth finally headed home.

"So what?" she shouted to the empty car. "So what if he's hanging out with a sophomore?" Todd was right. They were only sixteen. They had their whole lives ahead of them. *She* had her whole life in front of her. Not being with Todd meant she would have more time to spend with her friends and family, more time to do what *she* wanted to do.

Elizabeth parked the Fiat in the Wakefields' driveway. She slammed the door behind her and marched into the kitchen.

Jessica looked up with a smile of relief. "Where have you been?" she wanted to know. "I thought the car must have broken down again, so I started fixing dinner without you."

Elizabeth put her things on the table and helped herself to a glass of water. "No," she said grimly, "the car's just fine."

"Well, thank goodness you're home, that's all I can say." Jessica sighed. "I can't make any sense out of this recipe Mom left." She held up the index card. "What do you think she means by *sauté lightly?* I mean, how lightly? Just till it's hot, or till it's brown, or what?"

Elizabeth knew that there was no reason to take her bad mood out on her sister, but she did it anyway. "Who do I look like to you, Betty Crocker?" she snapped. "I'm just a teenager, too, you know. I'm not a professional chef or anything."

"You don't have to bite my head off," Jessica

shot back. And then she gave Elizabeth a long, hard look. "What's wrong, Liz?" she asked more gently.

Elizabeth picked up her things and started out of the room. "Nothing," she called over her shoulder. "I've just realized that I'm not busy tonight after all."

Later that evening, a little while before Sam Woodruff was supposed to arrive to take the twins to the movies, Jessica was painstakingly polishing her toenails Sunset Rose when the door to her room flew open and Elizabeth stormed in. "I can't find it!" she announced. "I've looked everywhere and I can't find it."

Jessica looked up, her brush poised. "Can't find what?" she asked.

"My journal!" Elizabeth shouted, as though Jessica should have known that was what she was talking about. "I've looked all over, and I can't find it anywhere."

"Well, where do you usually keep it?" she asked logically. "In your dresser? Under your pillow?"

Elizabeth flopped down on the foot of her sister's bed. "In my bag."

Jessica stared at her in open amazement. "Let me get this straight," she said slowly. "You carry your journal around with you in your bag? In public?"

Elizabeth nodded. "Yes, I do."

Jessica was still staring. "You take it to *school?* You take it to the *mall?*" She shook her head in disbelief.

"Well, you know," Elizabeth explained, "sometimes there's so much to write about that I can't get it all done at night. And I really hate to get behind, because it's so hard to catch up. So I bring it with me in case I get a chance to write in it during the day."

"You must be crazy," Jessica said. "I'd never do that. What happens if you lose your bag and some perfect stranger reads all about your life?"

"First of all," Elizabeth said, with a pointed glance around the mess of Jessica's room, "I'm not going to lose it. I take care of my things. And second of all, who'd be interested in reading about me?"

Jessica recapped the polish. "Well, I wouldn't argue with you about that." She smiled. "But the fact of the matter, Miss Neat and Orderly, is that you *have* lost it."

Elizabeth snapped her fingers. "No, I haven't." She grinned and sat up. "I just remembered. I was writing something in it in the library this afternoon, and I stuck it in the pocket of my jacket."

Jessica watched Elizabeth charge out of the room. "How can we be related?" she asked the cotton balls as she pulled them from between her toes. "It just doesn't seem possible."

Four

"Wasn't the movie last night hilarious?" asked Elizabeth.

Jessica nodded in agreement. "It *was* good." She reached across the table for the jam. She was feeling pretty pleased with herself. Not only had she managed to get Elizabeth to go to the movies with her and some of her friends the night before, but the evening had been an unqualified success. Elizabeth was looking happier and brighter that Friday morning than she had looked in days.

"Well," said Mrs. Wakefield, "it certainly sounds like you two had a good time."

"Oh, we did," said Elizabeth. "It's nice going to the movies with a lot of people." She sipped her juice.

"Did Todd and Sam like the movie, too?" Mr. Wakefield asked.

Jessica could see that this line of conversation

might lead to some questions her sister would rather not answer. "Yes," she said quickly.

"No," said Elizabeth at exactly the same time.

Mr. Wakefield looked puzzled. "Yes, Sam liked it and no, Todd didn't like it?" he asked.

Jessica could tell from her sister's face that her good mood had been broken. A second earlier she had been thinking about the fun they had had the night before. Now she was thinking about Todd.

Elizabeth picked up her dirty dish and glass. "Todd couldn't go," she said coolly. "He had something else to do." She stood up. "Come on, Jess. I promised Penny I'd be in early so we could go over the proofs for the next issue."

"You seem to be working especially hard lately," commented Mrs. Wakefield.

"Oh, you know Elizabeth," Jessica joked, jumping to her feet. "She's the only sixteen-year-old workaholic I know." She raised her voice. "We should get an early start, anyway," she announced with a glance in her father's direction. "Just in case the car breaks down again."

"I should have gone with you last night," said Enid as she and Elizabeth walked together to their first class. "It sounds like I missed a good time."

"You did," Elizabeth said. "Jessica and Sam's friends are really nice." She found herself looking involuntarily to either side as they crossed a corridor. The truth was that she was no longer feeling as enthusiastic as she hoped she sounded. She had had a good time the previous night, but ever since her father had asked about Todd it was as though she were being haunted by a ghost. And the awful thing was that this ghost wasn't alone. He had a companion. A giggling, pretty, dark-haired companion named Peggy.

She was suddenly aware that Enid was nudging her with her elbow. "Earth calling Elizabeth Wakefield," Enid was saying. "Please come in."

Elizabeth flushed. "Sorry," she said. "I guess I drifted off."

"I don't blame you." Enid laughed. "Hearing about how I did the laundry and glued back together a mug I'd broken isn't exactly absorbing."

"Wait a minute," said Elizabeth, finally managing to shove Todd's ghost and its companion out of her mind. "Is that all you did last night? Do laundry and repair a mug?"

"I did my homework, too," said Enid defensively.

"And that's all?"

"That's all? Liz, I had chemistry homework. Chemistry takes me forever."

"You mean you didn't call Hugh yet?" asked Elizabeth.

"Not exactly," Enid admitted.

"Not exactly?" Elizabeth repeated, unable to resist a teasing smile. "What does 'not exactly' mean?"

Enid groaned softly. "If you must know, it means that I picked up the telephone six times, that I dialed his number six times, and that each time I hung up after the first ring." She groaned again. "It was about a hundred times worse than chemistry."

"You're going to have to do better than that,"

chided Elizabeth. "You can't just give up now. I want you to promise me that you'll call him this afternoon."

Enid opened the classroom door. "I've changed my mind," she said. "I think I'm going to become a nun."

Elizabeth smiled. "But you're not Catholic, Enid. You can't become a nun."

"Yes I can," said Enid as she strode through the door. "I'll convert."

Jessica's heart sank when she pulled into the Wakefields' driveway that afternoon and saw that her mother's car was already in the garage. Elizabeth, not surprisingly, was staying late at school to work on the paper, but what Jessica had forgotten was that her mother had a dental appointment and was coming home early because of it.

The last thing she wanted was to be alone with her mother. Jessica knew that Mrs. Wakefield was becoming more and more curious about what was going on between Elizabeth and Todd. So far she had stopped short of asking anything directly, but it was obvious from the way she had watched Elizabeth at breakfast that she was about to start.

"Oh, no," she muttered as she turned off the engine. "Trapped by the Mother of the Million Questions."

She picked up her things and slid out of the car. There must be some way of avoiding having to tell her mother what was going on. Jessica concentrated. What was it army generals were always saying? A triumphant smile lit up her lovely face.

"That's it!" she said out loud. "The best defense is a strong offense!" Jessica shut the door of the Fiat, squared her shoulders, and marched to the back door.

Alice Wakefield was sitting at the kitchen table, having a cup of tea and reading the paper. She looked up as Jessica appeared in the doorway.

Jessica came in talking. "Mom," she said, "I know you don't believe me, but there really is something seriously wrong with that car. If you could have seen me on the way home! I practically had to get out and push it!"

"Why, good afternoon, Jessica," said Mrs. Wakefield. "And how are you? Have a nice day at school?"

"Fine," said Jessica. She threw her books on a chair and sat down across from her mother. "Mom," she continued, "listen to this. This is the absolute truth. You know that hill that leads up from the elementary school? Well, I was driving up it, and you know what? People were walking up as fast as I was driving. Little kids, Mom. Little kids were walking up that hill beside me. Not only that, but they were passing me."

"I'm glad to hear you don't drive too fast," said Mrs. Wakefield.

Jessica decided to ignore her mother's sarcasm. She leaned forward, her eyes wide with sincerity, her voice urgent. "It's not the speed that bothers me," she assured her. "It doesn't bother me that it's sluggish. It doesn't bother me that it's so dated. I don't even mind the fact that everybody at school has a better car than we do. But it's *undependable*. What if we get stuck somewhere at night? What if it makes us late for school? I hate to think of you sitting around worrying about us, Mom, because you don't know where we are or what's happened to the car."

"That's very considerate of you, Jessica," said Mrs. Wakefield.

Jessica decided to push what she saw as her advantage. "Especially around here, Mom. You know, because of the hills and the beaches and stuff. The truth is that the only kind of car anyone with any sense drives in southern California is a Jeep."

Mrs. Wakefield nodded. "A Jeep," she repeated. "I see."

"It's the only way to go, Mom," said Jessica. "They're dependable, they go anywhere. If we wanted to go camping in the mountains, if we needed to drive along the shore . . . Mom, have you ever tried to drive a Fiat Spider on sand?"

"No," said Mrs. Wakefield, gazing at her daughter over her mug. "No, oddly enough, I don't think I ever have."

"And that's not all, Mom," Jessica steamed on. "I mean, I know you're not really interested in appearances, but can you really say that it doesn't bother you to have your two beautiful daughters driving around in an old, broken-down car? Just think about it, Mom. It's practically a crime. It's like having this really fantastic dress and then wearing it to do the gardening. Can't you just imagine how great we'd look in a black Jeep with tinted windows and purple trim?" Exhausted, Jessica came to a sudden stop. She stared at her mother imploringly. Her mother stared back.

"And now I have a question for you," said Mrs. Wakefield.

"A Wrangler," said Jessica immediately. "It's the Jeep of my dreams."

"That wasn't the question," said Mrs. Wakefield. She put her elbows on the table and smiled pleasantly. "Jessica," she said gently, "the question was, what's going on between Elizabeth and Todd?"

Enid sat in her kitchen staring at the bright white telephone hanging from the wall. In front of her on the countertop was a pad and a pencil. Enid looked from the phone to the pad. She glanced at her watch. It was ten minutes later now than it had been the last time she had looked. Enid sighed again. She had promised Elizabeth that she would phone Hugh this afternoon, and she was determined to keep that promise. After all, Elizabeth was right. Hugh had seemed pretty glad to see her the other day. And although it had been a little awkward at first, once they had started talking it had seemed like the most natural thing in the world. Just like old times.

Enid looked down at the pad again. She had written her entire half of her telephone conversation with Hugh on it. That is, she had written her half of what *would* be her telephone conversation with Hugh if she ever managed to pick up the receiver and dial his number.

Enid read over what she had written. *Hi, Hugh, this is Enid. It was very nice seeing you the other day. I'll tell you the reason I'm calling. I think I may have lost one of my earrings in the café. The next time you go in there, do you think you could check for me? Thanks very much. I appreciate it. Bye.* It was all right, she decided. Then she thought of Jessica. No doubt Jessica would have come up with something amusing, interesting, and absolutely brilliant. She looked at her script again. It wasn't all right, it was awful. She picked up the paper and scrunched it into a ball, then tossed it into the wastebasket.

She had to practice, she decided. Jessica wouldn't need to practice, but she did. Enid took a deep breath. "Hi, Hugh," she said in a bright, high voice she didn't recognize. "This is Enid. Yeah, it was really nice to see you the other day. I enjoyed our talk. I guess you'd like to know why I'm calling. I'm missing one of my earrings, and I think that maybe I dropped it in the café. I was wondering if next time you were in there you could just see if anyone turned it in. You will? Oh, that's great, thanks a lot. Bye."

All she could hope for was that her voice didn't shake when she was talking to Hugh. Jessica's voice wouldn't shake, she figured. Of course, the other thing about Jessica was that she would have made the call about an hour ago.

At five twenty-seven she realized she could put it off no longer. Her mother would be home any minute, and she would never be able to phone him then. With a trembling finger, she punched the Grayson number. She caught her breath when it started to ring. *Just be calm,* she kept repeating to herself.

"Hello," said a voice she recognized as Mrs. Grayson's. "This is the Grayson household. No one is available to take your call at the moment. Please leave your name, number, and message at the tone."

Enid shrieked with joy. Hugh wasn't home! She didn't have to speak to him at all. She could talk to the answering machine instead!

The answering machine beeped.

"Hello," said Enid. "This is Enid. Enid Rollins. I'm calling for Hugh. I can't find one of my earrings—I mean, I think maybe I lost one of my earrings the other day. In the café. I mean, maybe I dropped it somewhere else, but I could have dropped it in the café. Anyway, if you ever go into the café again—I mean, don't go specially or anything, but if you do go in there, could you just see if they found my earring? Thank you. I'm sorry to bother you. This is Enid. Bye."

Enid hung up the phone and let out a sigh of relief. There, at least that was over. She had fulfilled her promise to Elizabeth *and* avoided speaking to Hugh at the same time. Even if he did ask at the café, she would never have to speak to him again. Because she hadn't really lost an earring, no one could have turned it in.

Enid had just begun to fix dinner when the telephone rang. "That'll be Elizabeth checking up on me," she said out loud.

She reached for the phone. "Hi," she grunted, trying to unscrew the top to the salad dressing at the same time.

"Hi," said a warm male voice. "Enid? This is Hugh."

Enid yelped as half a bottle of spicy Italian dressing went all over the floor.

* * *

The first thing Elizabeth had seen when she opened her eyes on Saturday morning was her sister. Jessica had been kneeling at the foot of Elizabeth's bed. "I've made a decision," she had announced. "This is a no-work day. You and I are going to the mall. We're going to look in windows, eat lunch, and spend money. And that's an order!"

Now, as they drove toward the Valley Mall, Elizabeth was glad that she had let her twin talk her into this expedition. She had spent quite a bit of time with Jessica over the last few days, and she had to admit that she was really enjoying herself.

Jessica started to sing. "A-shopping we will go, a-shopping we will go, get out the credit cards, a-shopping we will go . . ."

Elizabeth laughed. "Don't let Dad hear you singing that," she teased. "He has no sense of humor when it comes to you and spending money."

"I know," Jessica sighed as they pulled into the parking lot. "He's being really stubborn about the Jeep."

"Oh, come on, Jess," said her sister, linking arms as they began to walk toward the mall. "You don't really think Mom and Dad are going to buy us a Jeep, do you?"

Jessica tossed her head. "It may take a little persuading," she admitted, "but I'm sure they'll come around in the end." She gave a little skip as they sailed through the doors. "At the moment, though, I'll settle for a new outfit for the dance next week."

"You never give up, do you?" asked Elizabeth,

but her voice was filled with affection. "I'd completely forgotten there was a dance next week."

"Speaking of the dance . . ." said Jessica.

Elizabeth could tell from the casual tone of her sister's voice that she had some plan up her sleeve. "I wasn't speaking of the dance," Elizabeth pointed out. "I was just saying that I'd completely forgotten about it."

"Speaking of the dance," Jessica repeated, "Sam knows this really cute guy who's been asking to meet you—"

"No," said Elizabeth abruptly. "Don't even start."

"Why not, Liz?" Jessica squeezed her arm. "Sam says he's really nice, and you know what a good judge of character Sam is."

Elizabeth gave her sister a withering look out of the corner of her eye. She should have known Jessica wouldn't be able to wait too long before she started matchmaking. "Look, Jess," said Elizabeth reasonably, "Todd and I haven't even been separated for a week yet. I really don't feel that I'm ready to start seeing anyone else."

Jessica made an exaggerated face. "You're going to have to go out with someone else eventually," she argued. "You should give Sam's friend a chance. You don't have to marry him, Liz, you just have to dance with him for a couple of hours."

"No," said Elizabeth firmly. "It's too soon." It was true, of course, that she wasn't ready to start dating yet. But there was more to it than Elizabeth was willing to admit to Jessica. Foolish though it might be, she was still half hoping that Todd might ask her to the dance himself.

Jessica gave her sister's arm another squeeze.

"Why don't you just relax and start having a good time?" she urged.

"I *am* relaxing and having a good time," said Elizabeth truthfully. "And I'll go to the barbecue with you tonight, OK? But I'm just not ready to date, that's all."

They walked up the steps to the second level. "Liz," said Jessica as they strolled toward Bibi's, her favorite boutique, "there's something else I have to talk to you about."

Elizabeth turned to her sister. "Don't tell me," she kidded, "you've placed an ad in the personals for me."

But Jessica was looking very serious. Slowly, she met her sister's eyes. "It's Mom," she finally blurted out. "She cornered me in the kitchen yesterday, and made me tell her the truth about you and Todd."

Elizabeth sighed, but it was a sigh of resignation. She had known that their mother couldn't be kept in the dark forever.

"You're not mad at me, are you?" asked Jessica. "All I said was that you and Todd were in a kind of holding pattern."

Elizabeth put an arm around her sister's shoulder. "No, I'm not mad. I knew Mom was bound to find out sooner or later."

"That's the nice thing about fathers," said Jessica philosophically. "They give you money, and they compliment you when you look nice, but you're usually through your crisis before they even notice that you're having one."

Five

Elizabeth hummed an upbeat song as she go
ready for school on Monday morning. Not onl
had she survived her first Todd-less weekend, bu
she had really enjoyed herself. It had been so lon
since the twins had hung out together that Eliza
beth had forgotten how much attention the tw
of them could attract. Everywhere they had gon
in the mall on Saturday, heads had turned. Th
number of cute boys who had smiled or stoppe
to stare after them was nothing short of incredi
ble. Elizabeth winked at her reflection in the mir
ror. She had been part of a couple for so long tha
she had forgotten how many good-looking boy
there were in southern California. Just to remin
her again, there had been even more at the barbe
cue Saturday night. And on Sunday, when sh
and Jessica had gone to the beach to catch som
sun, there had been so many guys crowdin
around them that Jessica had joked that they wer

in more shade than if they'd brought an umbrella. Not that Elizabeth was interested in any of these boys. Just the same, it had made her feel good to think that they were interested in her.

Elizabeth studied herself in the mirror. She was wearing one of her favorite skirts and tops, but somehow the outfit looked a little dull. Jessica always dressed to be noticed, but Elizabeth's image tended to be more conservative. Maybe it was time to change that, she decided. She twisted a deep blue-green scarf through her hair. It brought out the color in her eyes. Elizabeth smiled at herself in the glass. Being sixteen, pretty, and unattached had its advantages.

Elizabeth was still humming as she sailed through the front entrance of Sweet Valley High. Perhaps it was only her imagination, but she couldn't help feeling that she was receiving at least one or two admiring glances. She held her head a little higher and smiled to herself. Out of the corner of her eye, she saw a tall, lanky boy, with short sandy hair and round steel-rimmed glasses, standing against the wall to her left. She could feel his eyes following her along the wall. It wasn't her imagination. She was definitely being watched. Without really meaning to, Elizabeth found herself turning her head in his direction. His good looks were quiet but intense, and she suddenly realized that she had noticed him before: he had been gazing at her at the Dairi Burger the night of Cara's going-away party. Their eyes met. Instantly, his rather serious face was transformed by a smile. Again without really meaning to, she found herself smiling back. *What is wrong with you?* she scolded herself. *You can't go around encouraging strange boys.*

"Liz! Liz!"

Elizabeth turned at the sound of her name. Much to her relief, Enid was racing toward her, waving frantically. *Saved,* she thought with relief.

"I've been looking all over for you," gasped Enid, grabbing hold of her arm. Her pretty face was flushed and her eyes were sparkling. "You're not going to believe what happened, Liz. You are just not going to believe it!"

Elizabeth couldn't get over how excited Enid seemed, especially considering how down she had been lately. "Try me!"

Enid leaned against the lockers. "Hugh found my earring!" she announced breathlessly. "Can you believe it?" she continued when Elizabeth didn't immediately respond. "He called me last night and said that he went back to the café and someone had turned it in!"

Elizabeth didn't respond immediately. She was thinking about the sandy-haired boy. She was sure that she knew his name, though she couldn't recollect it at the moment. He was a senior who belonged to a crowd of slightly offbeat, artistic types. She had an image of him sitting on the lawn, sketching in a notebook. What *was* his name?

Enid was almost shouting now. "Don't you think that's amazing?" she asked. "He *found* it!"

Elizabeth forced herself to concentrate on her friend. "That's great," she said with a bright smile. "That's really great. Did you arrange to meet him to pick it up?"

Enid snapped her fingers in Elizabeth's face. "Liz," she said, "would you mind telling me how Hugh could have found the earring I lost when I never lost one?"

"You what?" asked Elizabeth.

"I never lost one. Elizabeth, don't you remember?" Enid shook her head in astonishment. "Liz, it was your idea!"

"Oh, right."

"So what do you think it means?" Enid persisted. "How could he find something that never existed?"

Still sensing the tall, lanky boy behind her, Elizabeth thought for a second. "It's probably just a coincidence," she decided. "Someone else must have lost an earring, and Hugh just assumed that it was yours."

"Of course." Enid smiled. "That must be it." She pretended to fan herself. "Talk about luck!"

"You see," said Elizabeth, "it's fate that the two of you get back together."

"Maybe," Enid said, her smile losing a little of its brightness. "But maybe not. The trouble is, Hugh's training for a race in the park this afternoon, so I arranged to meet him there after school. Only this morning my mother told me that she has to go to Cold Springs after work, so I can't have the car."

"No problem," Elizabeth answered. "You can borrow the Fiat."

Enid gave her a hug. "Oh, thanks, Liz! I knew I could count on you! If I ever do get back with Hugh, I'll have you to thank."

"What are best friends for?" Elizabeth said as

they started down the hall. Unable to resist, she cast one last look behind her. The boy was still there, frozen in place, his eyes fixed on her.

At least things are working out for Enid, Elizabeth thought as she made her way to her locker before lunch. She couldn't think of anybody more deserving of a little good luck. Enid was one of the nicest people she had ever known. Loyal, honest, funny, intelligent . . . Elizabeth was busily recounting all of Enid's many fine qualities when someone suddenly jumped out at her from beside a staircase. It was too late for her to stop.

"Oof!" cried Elizabeth as the breath was knocked out of her. Her books and papers crashed to the floor of the nearly empty hall. "Oh, no," she cried as she dropped to her knees to begin gathering her belongings.

Elizabeth raised her eyes and saw the sandy-haired boy. All of a sudden she recalled his name: Kris. Kris Lynch. Every once in a while, *The Oracle* ran one of his cartoons. How could she have forgotten? And he always did the poster for the school play. Olivia Davidson, *The Oracle* arts editor, never got tired of praising his work.

He stooped beside her. Behind his glasses, his eyes were an amazingly dark, deep blue. "I'm—I'm really sorry," he stammered. "Are you OK?"

Elizabeth felt herself blushing. No wonder she had felt his eyes on her. He had the most intense stare, almost as though he were trying to see things that couldn't be seen. "Oh, I'm fine," she said hastily. "It was my fault. I wasn't looking where I was going."

She reached for her English notebook at the same moment that he did. Their fingers touched. They both pulled away so quickly that the notebook fell back to the ground.

Elizabeth got to her feet.

Kris Lynch picked up the notebook and handed it to her.

Neither of them moved. She was used to boys who were a little more talkative. She had a sudden, panicky thought that he was planning to stand there, just looking at her like that, for the rest of the lunch period.

"Well," said Elizabeth brightly, "it was nice running into you."

But just as she turned to walk away he touched her arm. "I was wondering if you'd want to go to the dance with me on Saturday," he said.

It was Elizabeth's turn to stare. She hadn't expected this. She knew he had been watching her, but any normal boy would introduce himself, chat, and get to know a little bit about her before he tried to make a date.

His blue eyes bored into hers.

Elizabeth's cheeks grew hot. She wasn't his type, she told herself. He wasn't her type. Even if Kris Lynch *had* been her type, she still couldn't go to the dance with him. What about Todd? She couldn't go with someone else when there was still a chance that Todd might ask her himself.

Elizabeth cleared her throat. "I'm . . . uh . . . I'm afraid I really don't know yet what my plans are for the weekend," she said. His expression didn't change. His eyes stayed fixed on hers. Why didn't he just nod and say *oh, sure,* like any other boy would?

Instead he handed her a small square of paper. On it was a pen-and-ink caricature of himself with some numbers written below it. The drawing was so clever that Elizabeth had to smile.

"It's my phone number," said Kris. "Maybe you could call me when you find out what you're doing."

Enid had spent most of lunch trying to convince Elizabeth to go out with Kris Lynch.

"What do you have to lose?" Enid had argued. "I know he's a little different and he doesn't talk much, but so what? He really is a fantastic artist, and a lot of girls think he's really attractive." She had given Elizabeth a knowing wink. "You have to admit he's got the most amazing eyes!"

But Elizabeth had admitted nothing. She had held to her line that she wasn't ready to start going out with someone new yet, especially when her separation from Todd was only temporary.

And now, as she waited at the Fiat for Enid after school, she was glad that she had. Coming toward her across the parking lot was none other than Todd himself.

"Elizabeth!" Todd called. "I want to talk to you."

Elizabeth's heart did a little skip. It was nice to know that she was pretty and popular, but it would be even nicer to know that the boy she thought was special felt the same way about her. And all at once Elizabeth was certain that that was what Todd was rushing over to tell her. He had had enough of their trial separation. He wanted her to go to the dance with him. How lucky that she hadn't let Jessica set her up with Sam's friend! How extremely lucky that she hadn't given in to Kris Lynch's deep blue eyes!

"Liz," gasped Todd, panting from his sprint across the lot. "I've been looking all over for you."

She tried to make her voice sound casual—normal and casual. "How are you, Todd?" She smiled. "I feel like I haven't seen you in days."

Todd nodded, his eyes on some spot just above her head. "Yeah," he said. "I've been kind of busy."

"Oh, so have I," said Elizabeth quickly. "I've hardly had a minute to think."

Todd jammed his hands into his pockets. "Liz," he said, moving his gaze to the bumper of the Fiat. "Liz, I don't know how to . . . I wanted to talk to you about the dance."

Elizabeth's heart tripped over itself. She was right! "Yes?" she said, unable to keep from smiling.

"Liz . . . you know how people talk. I didn't want someone else to tell you."

Elizabeth, on the verge of saying that of

course she would go with him, stopped herself just in time. "Tell me what?" she asked in a low voice.

Now he was staring at her feet. "Tell you that I'm going to the dance with someone else." In the silence, she could hear him breathing. He finally raised his eyes to her face. "With Peggy Abbot," he added. "I don't know if you know her or—"

She had to stop him from saying anything more. "What a coincidence," she said quickly. "I was looking for you to tell you that I've got a date for the dance, too. With a senior." She smiled her sunniest smile.

"With a senior?" Todd repeated, obviously taken aback.

"I'm sure you don't know him," said Elizabeth coolly.

"Well," said Todd, recovering his composure. "That's great, Liz, that's really great." He nodded several times. "You see how things are working out?" he said, giving her a tentative smile. "I knew this separation would be for the best."

"Oh, yes," agreed Elizabeth. "We should have done it long ago."

Enid was singing along with the radio as she drove to her meeting with Hugh. She turned off the main road and through the park entrance. She couldn't believe how well things were going—first running into Hugh at Moon Beach, and then having him actually seem happy to sit and talk with her. Then, best of all, the incredible luck of Hugh finding her "lost earring," so that they had to meet again. Maybe Elizabeth was right, and it was fated that she and Hugh would get back together after all.

Enid was so engrossed in her thoughts that it took her a couple of minutes to realize that she was slowing down. She glanced at the speedometer. The needle was moving steadily toward zero. She snapped off the radio. All she could hear was silence. *That's not right,* she told herself. *I shouldn't hear nothing, I should hear the engine.* With a honk of its horn, the car that had been behind her sped past. Enid put on her right turn signal and drifted to a stop at the side of the road.

For several minutes she just sat there. She was at least two miles from the gazebo, where she was supposed to meet Hugh in five minutes. Even a girl fueled by love could not run two miles in five minutes. She turned the ignition on and off. Nothing. She climbed out of the car and looked under the hood. In movies, there was always something in the engine that could be jiggled to get the car started again. But what? Enid shut the hood again and got back into the car. Elizabeth had warned her that the Fiat had been a little temperamental lately, but just dying like this struck her as a lot more than temperamental. Enid banged on the dash. "Come on!" she yelled. "Come on! Don't just sit here, get going!" Nothing happened.

Enid looked at her watch and moaned. Right at that moment, Hugh was probably coasting up to the gazebo. He was getting off his bike. He was leaning it against the building. He was sitting on the step. He was waiting . . .

Enid tried the ignition again. The Fiat made a tiny clicking sound, and then there was nothing.

Another image of Hugh, sitting on the steps of the gazebo, checking his watch, and wondering where she was, flashed through her mind. He would think that she had stood him up.

Enid started waving at passing cars, hoping someone would stop and give her a push. It was over an hour before a light gray station wagon came to a stop in front of the Fiat. Two small children and a Dalmation stared out the back at Enid. A pretty red-haired woman leaned out of the driver's window. "Need some help?" she asked.

In answer, Enid burst into tears.

Elizabeth sat at her desk, her journal open in front of her. What a day this had been! First Todd had dropped his bombshell about going to the dance with Peggy, and then Enid had gotten stuck in the Fiat and missed her meeting with Hugh.

She picked up her pen and began to write again. *So I called Kris Lynch and told him that I would go to the dance with him after all,* she wrote. *I wasn't sure he'd even know who I was, since we never exchanged names, but he said, "Gotcha," so I guess he did. I don't know—he seems nice enough, but the truth is that I'm not really interested in him. I'm not interested in him at all. The only boy I'm interested in is*

T. Elizabeth had to stop writing for a minute as her emotions overcame her. How could Todd just start going out with someone else like that, after all they had been to each other? A tear dropped to the open page of her journal. *What jerks boys are,* thought Elizabeth, suddenly furious. She wiped a second tear away and picked up her pen. *I'm sure Kris is just another jerk,* she wrote, *but at least it's only one date. It'll be over before I know it.* She threw the pen across the desk. Reading over what she had just written, Elizabeth realized that she was being unfair and taking her anger toward Todd out on Kris. "All he's done is ask you out," she scolded herself. "You can't call him a jerk for that!" She retrieved her pen intending to cross out the last two lines.

All at once, Jessica hurtled into the room, landing on the bed with a sigh. "Elizabeth," said Jessica, "Mom just told me what happened to Enid."

Elizabeth turned to see her sister gesturing toward the ceiling, very much as though she were impersonating the Statue of Liberty.

"We have got to have a serious talk about that car," said Jessica sternly. "Something has to be done."

"Something is being done," said Elizabeth. "I'm bringing it over to Jackson's right after school tomorrow."

Jessica shook her head. "That's not enough," she said. "Jackson's may fix the symptom, but they're not going to cure the disease. The Fiat is the disease, Liz. It's as simple as that."

Elizabeth let her pen drop to the desk. She closed her journal and pushed it aside. There was no point in trying to go on writing now. Jessica wanted to talk about the car, and that, Elizabeth knew, was what they would be doing for at least the next half-hour. "And I suppose *you* know what the cure is, right?" she asked.

"Of course," said Jessica. "A Jeep."

Leave it to Jessica to make her smile when she was feeling so down. "A Jeep?"

Jessica nodded. "Jet black with tinted windows and purple trim."

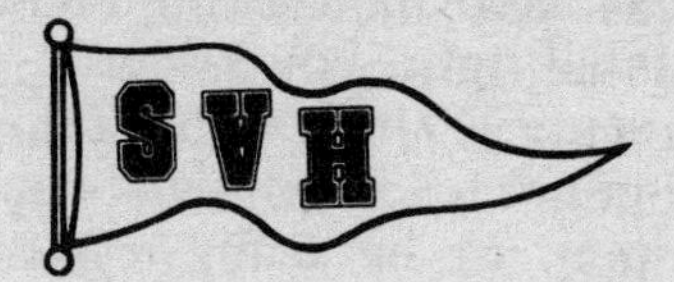

Six

"You never told me what Hugh said when you explained to him what happened yesterday," said Elizabeth as she steered the Fiat into traffic in the direction of Jackson's Garage.

Enid looked out the window. "That's because he didn't say anything," she said with a little laugh.

Elizabeth glanced over at her. "Nothing? You mean he was struck dumb by the horror of your terrible tale?"

She shook her head. "No, I mean I didn't tell him."

"What do you mean, you didn't tell him?" Elizabeth demanded. "Why not?"

"I just couldn't face him," Enid admitted. She shrugged. "The whole thing was simply too horrible for words, Liz. By the time I got home, I was so exhausted that I barely had the strength to cry." She leaned forward and switched on the radio. "And anyway," she continued, a little defensively, "he didn't call me, either. For all he knew, I'd been kidnapped by pirates and was halfway to Guatemala. He could have tried to find out if I was all right, you know."

"Enid," said Elizabeth in her calm, logical way, "you have got to tell Hugh what happened yesterday afternoon, or he really *will* think that you stood him up. What else could he think? He's not a mind reader, you know. He'll believe what he sees unless you tell him differently."

Enid turned to Elizabeth with a quizzical expression. "Oh, sure," she said, "just like you and Todd, right?"

Elizabeth checked the rearview mirror. "I don't know what you mean. The situation with Todd and me is completely different."

"Not that different," said Enid. "Todd has no idea how much you hate this separation. He has no idea how it drives you crazy that he's seeing Peggy. And he certainly doesn't know that you'd rather stay home and scrub mildew off the bathtub than go to the dance with Kris Lynch. So what can he do? Even if he wanted to call off the separation, he can't because now he thinks it's what you really want."

"*If* he wanted to call off the separation. It's pretty obvious that Todd is having the time of his life. As far as he's concerned, this separation is the best thing that could have happened."

"But that's just the point," Enid replied sternly. "You don't know that for sure. Todd could say exactly the same about you!"

"There, you see?" Elizabeth laughed. "That's

exactly why you should listen to my advice. You don't want to end up like me, do you?"

The first thing Enid did when she got home from Jackson's Garage that afternoon was check the answering machine. There was no message. To be more accurate, there were several messages, but none from Hugh.

Enid went into the kitchen to get herself a glass of water. "OK," she told herself as she took a glass down from the shelf, "you're going to call Hugh." She looked at the clock over the phone. It was just about the same time that she had called him the Friday before, which meant that he probably wouldn't be home. Enid's fluttering heart slowed down a bit. This was the perfect time to call him. She could tell her excuse to the machine. The machine couldn't hang up on her or give her a piece of its mind.

"Go for it, Enid," she said out loud. "Do it now!"

But Hugh picked up on the second ring. "Hello?" said that familiar voice.

Enid was so surprised that the only sound she could make was a croak.

"Hello?" Hugh repeated. "Who is this? Enid, is that you?"

She stared at the receiver. How did he know it was her? And then she started to laugh. If he had guessed it was her, then he must have been waiting for her call.

"Yes," said Enid, sounding almost normal, "it's

me. I wanted to explain about yesterday." The story came out in a rush. By the end of it, they were both laughing.

"I wondered what happened," said Hugh. "You see," he teased, "I always told you you should get a bike. They're much more dependable."

"They're also lighter," she said. "At least if I'd been on a bike, I could have picked it up and carried it when it broke down."

Hugh had one of the warmest laughs of anyone she had ever known. "*That* I would have liked to have seen—you coming across the park with the Fiat in your arms."

"How would you like to see me coming across the park *without* the Fiat in my arms?" She held her breath, amazed at her own boldness.

"Sounds OK to me," said Hugh. "How about Thursday, same time, same place—same earring?"

Enid couldn't feel the kitchen floor beneath her. She was floating over the black and white tiles, attached to the earth only by the cord of the phone. "Thursday," Enid repeated. "I'll see you then."

Lila arrived at lunch on Wednesday in a state of almost breathless hilarity. "You are not going to believe this," she announced as she sat down beside Jessica. "I've just heard the funniest thing. I mean, really, it took me five minutes to stop laughing."

Amy and Caroline, on the opposite side of the table, looked up. "Come on," Caroline urged. "Tell us. I could use a good joke."

"Me, too," said Amy.

Lila giggled. "Well, this is the best one yet," she assured them. She leaned forward, her eyes wide. "Listen to this! Someone just told me that Kris Lynch is taking Liz to the dance! Can you imagine? Kris Lynch and Elizabeth Wakefield? It's like the homecoming queen going out with the singer from a heavy metal band!"

"Oh, no," protested Amy. "Kris Lynch isn't like that. I think he's kind of cute."

Lila gave her sandwich a sniff. "He is kind of cute," she agreed, "in a moody, aloof sort of way. But Elizabeth isn't exactly his type, is she?" She rolled her eyes. "And he's certainly not hers." She shook her head. "I don't know what's happening to this school," she said in mock concern. "The gossip is becoming so unreliable."

Jessica jabbed her straw into her juice carton. Although she personally agreed that her sister and Kris went together about as well as apples and chili peppers, there was something about Lila's comment that made her feel she had to defend Elizabeth. "But it's true," she said quietly, turning one of her sweetest smiles on Lila. "Liz is going to the dance with Kris Lynch."

"What?" Lila gasped. "*Your* sister, Miss Perfect Teenager, is dating Kris Lynch, rebel with a paintbrush?"

Jessica nodded. "That's right. He practically begged her to go with him."

Lila threw her sandwich down on the table and leaned back in her chair. "I'm sorry," she said, "but I just can't believe this. Kris Lynch is eccentric. Everybody knows that. He's always drawing in his sketchbook and he's never played any sports. The only normal thing about him is that his father belongs to the country club."

Caroline smirked. "*Really,* Lila." She looked around the table, a broad smile lighting up her face. "Anyway," she added, her voice becoming conspiratorial, "I happen to know for a fact that Kris has been carrying a torch for Elizabeth for ages."

"Are you sure?" Lila asked, incredulous.

Even Jessica had a little trouble concealing her amazement at this announcement. "Who told you that?" she demanded.

Caroline's green eyes shifted evasively. "Common knowledge."

"Who?" Jessica pushed.

Caroline shrugged. "I heard it from someone who heard it from someone who knows Kris's sister. But he's really shy around girls like Elizabeth, and so he never even had the nerve to speak to her when Todd was in the picture."

"You're making this up," said Jessica.

Caroline shook her head. "I'm not making it up," she protested. "He really is in love with her. He even writes poems about her."

"Well, they must be short poems," said Lila. She made a face.

Jessica was too upset by this revelation even to snap back at Lila. She knew Elizabeth was going to the dance with Kris only because Todd was going with Peggy. She also knew that the last thing her twin needed at the moment was a boy who was serious about her. She bit her lip. Perhaps she should say something to Elizabeth about what Caroline had told her.

Jessica looked across the room to where her sister was sitting with Enid and Maria Santelli. At just that moment Todd and Peggy, deep in conversation, walked past their table. Someone who wasn't Elizabeth's twin sister wouldn't think that she had even seen them. But Jessica saw very clearly the pain in Elizabeth's eyes. *Let her go to the dance with Kris and have a nice time,* she told herself. *What difference is one date going to make? And anyway, if he really is crazy about her, it'll boost her ego.* Feeling a little better, she turned back to her friends.

"Well, you know what they say," Amy added. "Opposites attract."

"Amy," said Lila, flicking a few crumbs across the table, "when they say opposites attract they mean male and female, not Elizabeth Wakefield and Kris Lynch."

Thursday afternoon was sunny and bright. There wasn't a cloud in the sky. Nor was there any human form heading toward Enid from the horizon. She shifted her position on the steps of the gazebo and checked her watch.

He must have lost track of the time, she thought. *That can happen when you're riding, especially when you're trying to improve your speed.*

Enid checked her watch again.

Maybe he had been held up. Maybe he had run into some fellow racers and they had stopped to talk. It might be hard for him to get away.

Enid checked her watch yet again.

Could he have forgotten that they had agreed

to meet on Thursday? Could he have forgotten that they had said four-fifteen?

She checked her watch just one more time, holding it to her ear to make sure it was still running. It was. And four-fifteen had been quite a while ago.

"Hugh Grayson," Enid said out loud, "you've got ten minutes to get here before I never speak to you again as long as I live."

Just then, she caught sight of a small, dark shape hurrying over the hill. She jumped to her feet. She wondered if she had enough time to check how she looked in her mirror, but she decided that she probably didn't. *Sit down,* she told herself. *Be casual. You don't want to look too eager.* She sat back down. She pretended to be watching something in the opposite direction, very casually. A few minutes passed. Casually, she turned around again. It wasn't Hugh hurrying toward her, it was a large dog. And behind the large dog were a boy and a girl, walking slowly and holding hands.

Enid's jaw set. The couple stopped to exchange a kiss.

"He isn't coming," Enid said out loud. The instant she said it, she knew it was true. Hugh wasn't coming. He had never intended to come. He was paying her back for standing him up the other day. He had only been pretending to believe her story about the Fiat breaking down. Tears of humiliation stung her eyes. Only that morning she had been trying to work up enough courage to invite him to the dance Saturday night. What a fool she had been! She wiped away the tears with the back of her hand and got to her feet. Well, it was lucky that he hadn't turned up, then. Imagine how she would have felt if she had asked him out and he had laughed in her face!

Enraged and hurt, Enid stomped down the steps of the gazebo. She kicked a rock out of her way. "Love!" she yelled into the quiet of the park. "I'd rather be in algebra!"

Seven

Elizabeth was standing in the doorway to the bathroom, watching Jessica put on her makeup. "I suppose it really is too late to change my mind now," said Elizabeth glumly.

Jessica looked over her shoulder. "Yes," she said with an exasperated smile. "It really is too late." Elizabeth had been asking her this same question on an average of once an hour all day long. She tossed several tubes and pencils into a drawer and turned to her twin. "Elizabeth," said Jessica, "lighten up, will you? Kris is going to be here soon. Why don't you just relax and enjoy the dance?"

"I never should have said that I'd go with him." Elizabeth sighed. "I could have driven up to visit Steven. I could have stayed home tonight and worked on my English project."

"Not looking the way you do tonight," said Jessica. "Spending the evening with your lovelorn brother or a boring old novel? It would be a complete waste of a beautiful blonde!" She put her hands on her sister's shoulders and steered her out of the bathroom. "And anyway," she said firmly, "you did say you'd go. So you might as well enjoy yourself."

Elizabeth looked down at the floor. "But that's just it," she said in a whisper. "I don't think I can." She raised her eyes to her twin's. "Todd's going to be there with Peggy. You've seen them at school. They're going to be all over each other." She bit her lip. "I don't know if I can stand to be in the same room with them, Jess. I really don't."

Jessica slipped her arm through Elizabeth's and led her down the stairs. "That's all the more reason to go and have the time of your life," she said brightly. "You don't want to sit at home while Todd's having a good time with Peggy, do you? You don't want him to think of you as poor Elizabeth, who can't even get a date for Saturday night!"

Elizabeth shook her head. "Well, no, I guess I don't."

At the bottom of the stairs, Jessica, aware that Mr. and Mrs. Wakefield were in the living room, stopped and leaned close to her twin, mischief in her smile. "Have you ever heard Peggy's laugh, Liz?" she asked in a low voice. "She sounds like a donkey. You wouldn't want her to laugh at you, would you?"

"If she's going to laugh at me, I'd rather she did it when I wasn't there to hear her," said Elizabeth truthfully.

"But she's not going to laugh at you if you turn

up at the dance with a handsome senior on your arm," said Jessica. "And Todd's not, either."

Elizabeth had to admit that the thought of making Todd jealous cheered her up slightly.

"And besides," Jessica was saying, "it's only one date, Liz. It doesn't mean anything."

Outside, they could hear a car pull into the driveway. "There's Sam," said Jessica quickly. Suddenly, her eyes were bright with excitement, and she was in a hurry. "I've got to go." She gave Elizabeth a squeeze. "We'll see you at the dance!"

From the hall window, Elizabeth watched her sister run down the path. Sam was standing by the passenger door, ready to open it for Jessica. But Jessica didn't give him a chance. Instead, laughing happily, she threw herself into his arms and hugged him tightly.

The smile Elizabeth had been wearing for her sister's benefit vanished. She wished that she were looking forward to being with Kris one-hundredth as much as Jessica was obviously looking forward to being with Sam. Sighing heavily, Elizabeth leaned her head against the window. What had she done? Jessica's words came back to her. *It's only one date. It doesn't mean anything.* It was true, she told herself. It was one tiny, insignificant little date out of a life that would be filled with dates. A few months from now, she would look back on this night and laugh.

"What in the world is that?" asked Mr. Wakefield suddenly. "Is that a limo?"

"It looks like a chauffeur-driven Cadillac to me," said Mrs. Wakefield.

Elizabeth, deep in her own thoughts, thought

for a second that she must have misheard them. Who would be pulling up in front of their house in a chauffeur-driven Cadillac? She looked into the living room. Her parents were standing side by side at the window, staring out with amazed expressions on their faces.

"It isn't prom night, is it?" asked Mr. Wakefield.

His wife jabbed him in the ribs. "Of course it's not prom night," she said. "It must be Elizabeth's date for the dance."

"In a limo?" asked her husband.

"Look at that," breathed Mrs. Wakefield. "Not only does he have a limo, he has candy and flowers as well!"

Elizabeth watched as her father leaned closer to the glass. "Hey, wait a minute!" he exclaimed. "That's not Todd! What happened to Todd?"

Very, very slowly, and holding her breath, Elizabeth turned to look out the window near her. It was true. There was a gleaming pink Cadillac convertible parked directly in front of the house. And climbing out of the Cadillac, in an immaculate white suit, a bunch of pale pink roses in one hand and a pink, heart-shaped box of candy in the other, was Kris Lynch.

"Elizabeth!" her mother called. "Elizabeth! Your date's here!"

But Elizabeth couldn't move. Step by step, she watched Kris come toward the house. She had never seen him dressed up before, and she had to admit that the effect was incredible. He looked almost like a movie star. She also had never seen him looking so happy before. Tonight his blue eyes were sparkling with excitement.

The doorbell rang.

"Elizabeth!" Mrs. Wakefield called. "Are you there?"

Elizabeth managed to find her voice. "Yes," she said, "I'm here."

Kris, suddenly seeing her looking at him through the window next to the door, raised the flowers in greeting.

She waved back.

"Elizabeth!" her mother was shouting now. "Answer the door!"

Elizabeth reached for the knob. *Someday,* she told herself, *you are going to laugh about this. But not tonight.*

"This has always been my fantasy," Kris told her as the Cadillac glided through the streets of Sweet Valley.

Elizabeth smiled. "Going to a dance?" As awful as she was sure this night was going to be, she was relieved that it had finally begun.

Kris laughed. He had a nice laugh. "Sort of," he said. He leaned back against the white leather seat. "Going to a dance with a beautiful California blonde in a pink Cadillac on a warm, starry night," he said softly. "That's the fantasy." He turned to her with a smile. He had a nice smile, too. "And here we are. I can't believe it."

"I can't believe it, either," said Elizabeth. She could only hope that he didn't realize that what was a fantasy for him was something of a nightmare for her. This was not just one date to him. It was special. It meant something.

* * *

The Cadillac came to a halt in front of the school. Elizabeth looked over at the familiar building. Its lights were burning brightly, and the sounds of music and laughter drifted across the rolling lawn. She took a deep breath. Here was the moment she had really been dreading. *Stop it!* she ordered herself. *Todd will be with Peggy, and that's all there is to it. You don't have to talk to them. You don't even have to look at them if you don't want to. Just go in there and have a good time!* She took Kris's arm.

"I have a confession to make," he whispered as they walked toward the entrance.

"What's that?" asked Elizabeth, her eyes darting warily among the other couples heading to the dance.

"Well, the truth is, I'm a little nervous. I've never actually been to one of these dances before." He squeezed her hand. "I'm glad I'm with you."

Elizabeth didn't want to hear how glad he was to be with her, but she did want to say something reassuring. *Don't worry, Kris, there's nothing to be nervous about. We're going to have a good time.* But as they stepped through the doorway the words died in her throat. There, not two feet in front of them, were Todd and Peggy. "Todd!" she cried in surprise.

Todd swung around. "Elizabeth!" For a second, he just stared at her, in very much the way that she was staring at him. And then his eyes shifted to Kris.

To hide her confusion, Elizabeth pulled Kris forward. "Kris," she said quickly, "I'd like you to meet Todd Wilkins. Todd, Kris Lynch." She looked at Peggy. There was no way she was going to admit that she remembered her name.

"And this is Peggy Abbot," said Todd. "Peggy, Elizabeth and Kris."

Elizabeth and Kris, Elizabeth repeated to herself. The words went through her like a cold blade.

Kris extended his hand. "Nice to meet you," he said.

Peggy giggled. Jessica had been right. She did sound like a donkey. A donkey that was being tickled.

Peggy giggled again. "I've heard so much about you," she said to Elizabeth. "Of course, I see you around school a lot. You look just like your sister, don't you?"

Out of the corner of her eye, she could see Kris's mouth twitch with the effort of not smiling. "We're twins," said Elizabeth evenly.

This time Peggy didn't giggle, she tittered. "I guessed you were," she said. "I mean, sometimes it's hard to tell you apart, isn't it?"

Elizabeth tried to catch Todd's eye, but he was staring intently at Peggy's ear. "Not really," said Elizabeth sweetly. "I'm the older one."

Todd started edging Peggy away. "We'd better get going, Peggy," he said to her. "Everyone will wonder what's happened to us."

"Isn't that amazing?" Peggy said to Todd as he shuffled her away. "She doesn't really look older, does she?"

* * *

Elizabeth couldn't talk, she couldn't dance, she couldn't think. All she could do was stare across the room at Todd and Peggy. Every time Todd put his arm around Peggy, Elizabeth felt it. Every time Peggy laughed, Elizabeth heard it. Every time Todd leaned over to say something to Peggy, Elizabeth knew it must be about her. *He's telling her he thinks she's prettier than I am,* she thought. *He's telling her that he's glad he isn't with me anymore. This is not a trial separation. This is for good!*

She knew that Kris was trying to get a conversation going with her, but she was powerless to help him. How could she be expected to join in on small talk when every cell in her body was concentrating on the smiling couple at the other side of the auditorium?

And then Todd and Peggy disappeared behind a group of dancing couples. Elizabeth moved to the other side of Kris, who was gamely talking to her about music. She still couldn't catch a glimpse of them. "Why don't we get some punch?" Elizabeth suggested, thinking that she might be able to see them from the refreshment table.

Kris looked a little surprised that this sudden request had come in the middle of something he had been saying about Elvis Presley, but he nodded happily. "Sure," he said. "Sounds good to me."

Elizabeth resumed breathing. Todd and Peggy were in view again. *What does he see in her?* she wondered. *Peggy's cute, but she seems so silly and frivolous. He can't really be serious about her, can he?*

"You know," said Kris, handing her a glass, "I always read your articles in *The Oracle*. They're the best things in it." He smiled at her. "You're a terrific writer, you know. You really are."

Elizabeth, dimly aware that some response was required of her, said, "Oh . . . um, thanks."

Kris touched her arm. "Elizabeth," he said, giving her a little shake. "Are you all right? I don't think you've heard a word I've been saying."

Elizabeth blushed. "I'm sorry, Kris," she said sincerely. "I guess I was daydreaming."

"Well, I know what that's like," he answered with a little laugh.

I guess I owe him a second date. He made such a big deal out of the dance, Elizabeth was writing in her journal. *I mean, if someone picks you up in a pink Cadillac, the least you can do is go to the movies with him, even if it is just because you have nothing better to do. And anyway, maybe Todd will get jealous if he hears that I'm really going out with someone else. I—*

Elizabeth broke off as her sister practically flew through the door of her room.

"I don't believe it!" squealed Jessica. "I just do not believe it! He picked you up in a pink Cadillac convertible! Everybody was talking about it! I've never seen anything so cool! Sam spent most of the night wishing he could just drive it around the block!"

Elizabeth wished she could share some of her twin's enthusiasm. "To be honest," she said, "I think he went a little overboard. Did you happen to notice the flowers and candy downstairs?"

Jessica nodded. "He is so romantic!" she sighed. "Sam's idea of sweeping a girl off her feet is to dedicate a race to her." She bounced down next to her twin. "Well?" she demanded. "Are you going to tell me, or do I have to drag it out of you? Did you have a good time? Was he nice? Can he dance? Did it drive Todd wild to see you with such a good-looking guy?"

Elizabeth shrugged. "It was all right."

"All right?"

"Uh-huh."

"That's it? He carries you off to the dance like the prince picking up Cinderella, and all you can say is, it was all right? Does he have bad breath or something?"

"No," said Elizabeth, "he doesn't have bad breath. In fact, he's a very nice boy. And he's intelligent. I don't always understand what he's talking about, but he's definitely all right."

Jessica made a face. "If you don't understand what he's talking about, it's probably because you don't listen to him." She fixed her sister with a stony stare. "I saw you, Elizabeth Wakefield," she told her, "following Todd and Peggy around all night with your eyes."

Elizabeth groaned. "I couldn't help it, Jess," she confessed. "It was awful. Absolutely awful. Kris really is nice, but the problem is that he isn't Todd. Everything he said or did, I compared to what Todd would have said or done." She groaned again. "It wasn't so bad when we were dancing—then he was happy because we were together, and I was happy because I didn't really have to talk to him—but the rest of the time it was a disaster."

"Oh, well," said Jessica, kicking off her shoes.

"So you got to ride in a pink Cadillac, and now you'll never see him again."

Elizabeth's cheeks turned pink. "Well, actually," she mumbled, avoiding her sister's curious stare, "I did say I'd go to a movie with him next week."

"You what?"

"He asked me on the way home. We were sitting in the car, and the radio was on, and there were all these stars twinkling above us . . ."

"And then what?" asked Jessica, sitting up straight. "He put a gun to your head and said you had to go out with him again?"

Elizabeth leaned against her sister. No matter how miserable she felt, Jessica was the one person who could always make her smile. "I think it was just that I was so surprised he wanted to see me again after the way I'd treated him all night that I said yes before I could figure out how to say no."

A concerned expression came over Jessica's face. "But if you don't like him, Liz, why lead him on?"

Elizabeth blinked. "Are *you* lecturing *me* about leading people on?" she asked indignantly. "*You*, of all people?"

"Liz," explained Jessica calmly, "it's different when I do it. Everyone expects me to act like that. I'm a flirt. But they don't expect it from you. It's like being lied to by George Washington."

Elizabeth closed her eyes. "Please don't make me feel worse than I already do," she begged. "I just couldn't help myself.

"Well, it's not too late," said Jessica briskly. "You still have time to change your mind."

Eight

"Jessica," said Elizabeth irritably, "would you please hurry? I'd really like to get to school a little early this morning."

Jessica removed another handful of objects from her bag. "They're in here somewhere," she said grimly. "I know they are. Yesterday was Sunday, and I used the car in the afternoon . . ."

"Don't tell me you two are taking the Fiat," joked Mr. Wakefield. "I thought you'd be going in Elizabeth's pink Cadillac from now on."

Elizabeth winced. Ever since Kris had picked her up for the dance, her parents had been dropping hints. She knew that they were curious to know what was going on, but she was trying to forget Saturday night, not remember it. Fortunately, right at that moment Jessica pulled a wad of tissues, ribbons, and candy wrappers from her bag. She shook it and it jangled. "Here they are!" she cried. "You see, I knew I had the keys."

"Great," said Elizabeth, already halfway through the door, "let's go."

"You're in a big hurry this morning," said Jessica as she started the car. "You have another meeting for the paper or something?"

Elizabeth sighed. "Or something," she said, looking over at her twin. "I've decided you're right about Kris. There's no point in going out with him when I know I'm not really interested."

"Especially when he *does* seem to be interested," Jessica added.

"Exactly," agreed her sister. "He'll think I'm encouraging him, when all I'm doing is being polite. And then I really will have a mess on my hands."

Jessica turned down the road to Sweet Valley High. "Take it from one who knows," she said with a laugh. "It's always better to quit while you're ahead."

Encouraged by her sister's advice, Elizabeth marched purposefully into the school. She would wait at Kris's locker until he showed up, and then she would tell him as nicely as possible that she had changed her mind about seeing him again. She would make sure that he understood that it wasn't because of him. She liked him, she really did. But she couldn't go out with him.

Elizabeth turned the corner and caught her breath. There, standing against the wall, was Todd. His arms were filled with books, and he was anxiously looking up and down the hallway.

His eyes fell on Elizabeth. It was obvious from his expression that he had not been looking for *her*.

Elizabeth's first instinct was to turn right around and go back in the direction she had come from. But then she realized how silly that was. Here she was on her way to tell Kris that she couldn't go out with him because she still had feelings for Todd, but every time she saw Todd she wanted to run. She forced her lips into a smile. She and Todd just had to get over this awkwardness with each other, Elizabeth decided.

"Hi, Todd!" she called brightly.

"Oh, hi, Liz," he answered lamely. His eyes were looking everywhere but at her.

She came to a stop right beside him. "How are you?" she asked, amazed at how normal her voice sounded. "It seems like ages since we've seen each other."

Todd nodded, smiling sheepishly. "Well, we did see each other Saturday night," he reminded her.

Really, thought Elizabeth, *does he think I've forgotten? He must know that the sight of him with his arms around Peggy is forever burned into my brain.* But aloud what she said was, "Oh, sure, we *saw* each other. But I meant to talk." She made her smile brighter. "You know . . ."

Todd looked back at her blankly. He cleared his throat. "Well, I've been pretty busy lately, what with one thing and another, and—"

"How about lunch today?" she asked, interrupting him. "It'd be really nice to have a chat. After all, we *are* still friends, aren't we?"

Todd's eyes shifted uneasily. Elizabeth was sure he was expecting Peggy to arrive at any second. "Yeah, sure we are," he mumbled. "Of course. And I'd really like to have lunch with you, Liz, but . . . well, I sort of promised Peggy that I'd eat with her and her friends today."

Elizabeth was about to argue that he always ate with Peggy and her friends these days, but just in time she remembered that it had been a statement like that that had caused their separation in the first place.

"Maybe some other day," said Todd. "Maybe next week or something."

Elizabeth's cheeks were burning. *Maybe next week or something?* How could she have allowed herself to be humiliated like this? Todd had no intention of eating lunch with her. He certainly had no intention of remaining friends. "Sure," said Elizabeth. "Next week. That sounds great."

All Elizabeth wanted to do was get away from Todd before Peggy did show up. She turned back to the corridor. At the other end of the hall, Kris Lynch was striding toward her. An honest, delighted smile lit up his face at the sight of her. Elizabeth smiled back. *I'll show you, Todd Wilkins,* she thought. *Don't think that you're the only fish in the sea.* "Kris!" she called, a little more loudly than she had planned. "I've been looking for you!"

She could feel Todd's eyes on her back as she ran down the hall and took hold of Kris's arm.

Enid was spending her Monday lunch period filling Elizabeth in on the latest developments in

Operation Hugh Grayson. Hugh had called her on Friday afternoon, just as she stormed into the house, but she had told her mother to tell him that she wasn't home yet. He had called twice on Saturday, but again she had told her mother to say she was out. Enid's mother thought that she should find out what he had to say, but Enid was afraid of making a fool of herself again.

"So you see," Enid was saying to Elizabeth, "now I'm right back where I started. I still don't know what to do."

Elizabeth looked up from listlessly stirring her yogurt. "About what?" she asked. Elizabeth had positioned herself at the lunch table so that she couldn't see Todd sitting with Peggy and her friends, but she knew they were there. All the while Enid had been talking to her, she had actually been listening for the sound of Todd's laugh or his voice saying someone else's name.

Enid sighed. "Liz," she said patiently, "I know you've got a lot on your mind, but could you just pretend to pay attention to me for a few minutes?"

"Just tell me what they're doing," said Elizabeth.

Enid peered over her friend's head. "She's feeding him," she informed her, wrinkling her nose in disgust. "It's really gross, believe me. You're right not to watch."

"I can't believe it!" hissed Elizabeth. "Todd's letting her *feed* him?"

"Well, not with a spoon or anything," Enid amended. "But she is putting potato chips into his mouth." She sighed again. "Maybe I should do nothing about Hugh. Maybe I'd be a happier, healthier person if I just forgot about love completely."

The sound of Peggy's laugh, which today reminded Elizabeth more of a cross between a squealing pig and a vacuum cleaner than a donkey, bounced through the cafeteria.

"Oh no you don't," said Elizabeth to Enid quickly. "You follow your heart." She winked. "After all," she said, "why should I be the only one to feel this bad?"

It was another quiet afternoon at the Rollinses' home, and Enid was spending it staring at the telephone, wondering whether to call Hugh or not. She decided to toss a coin. Heads, she'd call him; tails, she wouldn't call him. She fished a quarter out of her pocket, closed her eyes, and threw it into the air. It came up tails. She decided to call Hugh anyway.

It wasn't until the answering machine came on that she remembered that Hugh had told her he wasn't home on Monday afternoons, when he worked in a bike shop in Big Mesa. She hung up the receiver and looked at the clock. Now what? It seemed a shame to quit now, when she had gotten this far.

It was then that Enid had her idea. Her mother had left her the car that afternoon so Enid could pick up some groceries for dinner. Food, Enid reasoned, was sold everywhere, even in Big Mesa. If she drove there for the shopping, then she could just drop in on Hugh to say hello as long as she was in town. "Yes," Enid announced to the kitchen, "that's what I'll do." Relief flooded through her. At last she was going to see Hugh again. Seeing him, she told herself as she hurried out to the car, was better than not seeing him, no matter what happened.

As soon as she walked through the door to the bike shop, Enid realized that she had been wrong. Seeing the boy she loved *was* better than not seeing him if when she did see him he was heaving an Italian racer up onto his shoulder or pumping up a tire. But that was no longer true if he was standing in a darkened corner with his arms around a slender redhead, as Hugh was at that moment.

Hugh looked up just in time to see the stricken look on Enid's face. "Enid!" he yelled.

Enid spun around, yanked the door open so hard that the glass rattled, and raced into the street as though there were wild dogs after her. Behind her she could hear Hugh shouting at the top of his lungs, "Enid! Wait a minute! Enid! Come back!" She didn't turn around.

The first thing Enid did when she got home was phone Elizabeth.

"She was wearing his ring on a chain around her neck," Enid sniffled. "The same ring I used to wear."

"I thought you said she was pressed against him," said Elizabeth. "How could you see that she was wearing his ring?"

"She pulled back," choked Enid. "So he could kiss her."

Elizabeth's voice was gentle and reasonable. "Enid, I thought you said you got only a very quick look at them before you ran out of the store."

"It was quick," Enid explained, "but it was intense."

"You're sure you're not exaggerating just a little?"

Enid dried the last few tears away with a paper napkin. "Of course not. I know exactly what I saw." She leaned against the refrigerator. "That does it," she groaned. "I'm locking myself in my room until the convent has an opening."

"Just remember one thing," Jessica warned Elizabeth as she got ready for her second date with Kris on Tuesday night. "If you spend all your time comparing the boy you're with to the boy you used to be with, you'll never meet anyone new."

"I wouldn't do that," said Elizabeth.

"Oh, sure you wouldn't," said Jessica, sounding exasperated.

But even though Elizabeth had believed herself at the time, the first thought that came into her mind when she opened the door to him was, *Todd would never dress like that.*

"Hi." Kris smiled.

He was wearing a plain black T-shirt, faded jeans, and a small silver hoop in his left ear. Elizabeth hadn't noticed before that he wore an earring.

"You look surprised," he continued. "Our date *is* for tonight, isn't it?"

"Oh, yes." Elizabeth nodded. "It's tonight." She returned his smile. "It's just that you look so . . . so different." *From Todd,* she added silently.

The deep blue eyes were amused. "I dress up for dances," he said. "This is normal."

He pointed behind him, to where a customized bright green Volkswagen Beetle stood by the curb. "No pink Caddy, either." He grinned. "But I promise to buy you popcorn for the movie."

"Great," said Elizabeth with genuine feeling. She could relate to popcorn. Popcorn was something Todd always bought. "I'll just get my jacket."

He reached out to stop her. "Wait a minute," said Kris. "There's something I've got to tell you."

He might not look anything like Todd, Elizabeth thought, but he did have a remarkable smile. "What is it?"

"You look really lovely tonight."

Elizabeth had been too upset the night of the dance to pay any real attention to Kris. But that night she decided to make it up to him. As they drove to the movie theater she asked him about himself. Where did he live? Did he have any brothers and sisters? Had he customized the VW himself? Who were his teachers? What were his plans for the future? Knowing his reputation for being a little different, she somehow hadn't expected him to be as shy as he was.

"Hey, hold on." He laughed. "The other night you barely spoke to me at all, and tonight you won't stop asking me questions." He watched the traffic with a serious expression. "I'm not really used to talking about myself."

"I didn't mean to pry," Elizabeth apologized. "I guess it's just that I'm feeling nervous."

"You're feeling nervous?" he inquired as he turned toward town. He looked over at her. "Can you keep a secret?" he asked.

Elizabeth nodded.

"I've never really gone out with a girl like you before," he confessed. "I've never taken one to a movie and bought her popcorn. I'd never been to a dance like the one the other night. I've never gone bowling. I've never even been to a football game."

"Well," said Elizabeth at last, "what *do* you do?"

He came to a stop at a light. "I paint and I draw," he said, his eyes on her.

Kris and Elizabeth talked about their work for *The Oracle.* He was also full of funny, fascinating stories about famous artists and artworks. Elizabeth, without quite realizing how she got on to the topic, found herself telling Kris all about her dreams to be a professional writer someday.

"I knew it," he said as they came out of the theater. "I could tell from reading your articles in the school paper."

"Really?" asked Elizabeth, feeling unexpectedly pleased.

"Sure. You're a natural." He came to a stop in

the middle of the street. "OK," he said, "we've gone to the movie, we've eaten the popcorn. Now what do we do?"

Elizabeth was suddenly aware that she was having a good time. "We go to the Dairi Burger," she told him happily.

It wasn't until they walked into the Dairi Burger that Elizabeth realized she hadn't thought of Todd once in the past two and a half hours. For two and a half hours she had been feeling completely normal, but now that feeling was shattered. Because there, sitting at a table near the front, was Todd Wilkins. And beside him, blowing her straw wrapper in his face, was Peggy Abbot. They seemed to be having a wonderful time. *If Peggy sat any closer to Todd,* thought Elizabeth, her bones beginning to ache with jealousy again, *she'd be on his lap.* Without a second thought, she slipped her arm through Kris's. The smile he turned on her was surprised but pleased. "Let's sit at the back," said Elizabeth in a loud, clear voice. "Where we can have some privacy."

"Remember when you asked me before what it is I do?" Kris asked as they slipped into a corner booth.

Elizabeth, looking to see if Todd was looking, nodded vaguely.

"Well, there is one other thing I do," said Kris.

"What's that?" asked Elizabeth, not really listening.

"I think about you."

* * *

Sam was working on his bike Tuesday evening, so Jessica had stayed in. She had talked on the telephone, tested out several new shades of nail polish, and spent enough time doing her homework to feel that she deserved a medal. Now, bored and restless, she had joined her parents in the living room, where she had resumed her campaign for a new car.

"But Dad," Jessica was arguing, "fixing the Fiat is just throwing good money after bad. Sure it's working now, but how long is that going to last? It's old, Dad, it's had its day."

"Is that what you're going to say about me in a few years?" teased Mr. Wakefield. "He's had his day, let's replace him with a Jeep?"

"Dad," Jessica wheedled, "I'm not thinking of myself. I'm thinking of you."

Mr. Wakefield held up his hands. "Please," he pleaded, "credit me with some intelligence, will you, Jessica? If you want a new car, it isn't because you're thinking of me. It's because you've seen something in the exact color you've always wanted, and you've already picked out what you're going to wear when you drive it."

"Dad—" Jessica began, but stopped as the front door opened and Elizabeth came in.

"Elizabeth!" Jessica cried. "Help me make Dad see reason about the car."

Elizabeth put her things on the hall table. "You're on your own tonight," she said with a smile. "I'm exhausted. I'm going to bed."

She was back only a few minutes later, looking

for her journal. "I've got so much to write, and lately I'm always forgetting where I leave it."

"It's amazing, isn't it?" asked Jessica as Elizabeth disappeared back up the stairs. "You wouldn't think someone like Elizabeth *had* anything to put in a journal. 'Dear Diary, Today I went to school. I got another A. I wrote another article for *The Oracle.* I went home and did my homework.' "

"How about this?" asked Mr. Wakefield. " 'Dear Diary, Tonight my father said he is absolutely not going to buy us a new car, no matter how much Jessica nags, moans, or begs.' "

Nine

Jessica had a long telephone conversation with Lila on Thursday night, most of it about Elizabeth.

"It's driving me crazy," Jessica confided to Lila. "People I hardly know are starting to ask me about them. One or two have even told me what an interesting couple Elizabeth and Kris make!"

"You know what people are like," said Lila in a bored voice. "They love to talk because they have nothing better to do."

Jessica didn't point out that Lila was one of the worst gossips she knew. Instead, she said, "Elizabeth's going to be a little upset when she finds out that everyone thinks that she and Kris are a couple."

Lila laughed. "Kris is going to be even more surprised when he finds out that they're not."

"What are you talking about?" asked Jessica.

"Oh, come on, Jess," said Lila. "You know what Caroline said about Kris having a crush on Liz. Anyway, he's been telling his friends that he and Elizabeth are practically going steady."

"They've had a few dates," said Jessica.

"Um," said Lila, sounding far from convinced. "And three lunches, two library sessions, two long walks, at least a dozen meetings in the hall, *and* he drove her home after school yesterday."

Jessica, sitting on her bed, collapsed against the pillows with a groan. *It's too bad that Lila is more interested in shopping than in international politics,* she thought, *because she'd make a great spy.* "He drove her home because *I* needed the car," said Jessica indignantly. "You know that, Lila. You were with me."

"Oh, sure," said Lila. "I know that because I'm your best friend. But how do you think it looks to everyone else? All they see is Elizabeth and Kris hanging out together all the time. You don't really think anyone's going to assume that they're just good friends, do you?"

Jessica kicked a sandal off the bed. Sometimes it really annoyed her when Lila was right. "If you want to know what I think, I think it's not really anybody else's business," she snapped.

"No," said Lila sweetly, "but it is Kris Lynch's business. And no one's told him that he and Elizabeth aren't a couple."

Jessica sighed. She knew Elizabeth wasn't trying to lead Kris on, but she also knew that she wasn't trying too hard to discourage him either. This was partly because she liked him and didn't want to hurt his feelings, and partly because she was so upset about Todd. "Well, someone's going to," Jessica decided. "And soon."

Friday morning, Jessica woke up with one thought in her mind: talk to Elizabeth about Kris.

But she quickly discovered that talking about Kris wasn't something Elizabeth wanted to do.

"Really, Jess," said Elizabeth as they drove to school, "I appreciate your concern, but there's nothing to worry about. Kris and I are just friends."

"Maybe that's what you think," insisted Jessica, "but everybody else thinks—"

Elizabeth shook her head. "I'm not interested in what everybody else thinks," she said sharply. "Let them think whatever they want."

"But what about Kris? Don't you care what he thinks?"

Elizabeth glanced at her twin. "Of course I do," she said quickly. "But we've only had a few dates, Jessica. It's not like we've kissed or anything. There's no chemistry between us. And I'm sure Kris knows that."

Jessica leaned back in her seat, her arms folded across her chest. "Don't count on it," she advised her sister. "Just because you don't feel a spark doesn't mean he's not building a bonfire."

"Sometimes I think you're the one who should be the writer." Elizabeth grinned. "You have such an imagination."

* * *

"It's so weird," Enid was saying to Elizabeth at lunch. "All of a sudden, everywhere I go, I run into Hugh. I even bumped into him in the stationery store the other day." She gave an exaggerated groan. "Why now, when I never want to see him again as long as I live?"

Elizabeth smiled sourly. "Tell me about it," she answered. "I can't walk down the corridor without tripping over Todd and Peggy."

Enid pointed a cucumber spear at her friend. "Yeah, but it's understandable that you'd run into them. I mean, they live in the same town and go to the same school. Hugh has to go a little out of his way to do his shopping in Sweet Valley, Liz."

"True." Elizabeth laughed. Then she asked, more seriously, "Have you talked to him since you saw him with that girl?"

Enid rolled her eyes in horror. "Are you kidding? I felt like such a fool! There's nothing I could say to him." She bit into the cucumber, chewing thoughtfully. "What about you? Have you told Kris yet that you're not really interested in him?"

"Not you, too!" Elizabeth sighed. "I had Jessica on me all the way to school. She seems to believe that everybody thinks we're already a couple."

"Maybe you should listen to her," suggested Enid. She stared intently at her sandwich for a few seconds. "To tell you the truth," she finally went on, "a few people have asked me if you and Kris are serious."

"But that's ridiculous," Elizabeth protested.

"Who would be dumb enough to think that after we've had only a date or two?"

Before Enid could answer, however, Maria Santelli rushed up to their table. "Enid," she said, looking down at a list in her hand, "I just wanted to make sure you're coming to my party tomorrow night."

"Hey, what about me?" bantered Elizabeth. "Don't you want to know if I'm coming?"

"Oh, *you*." Maria grinned. "I know you're coming. Your boyfriend already told me."

Elizabeth could feel Enid looking at her, but she was too shocked to do more than stare at Maria. "My boyfriend?" she repeated.

"Sure," Maria said, nodding. "Your boyfriend, Kris." She laughed awkwardly. "It sounds strange, doesn't it? I still can't get used to the idea that you're not with Todd anymore. Still," she said with a shrug, "I guess that's life, isn't it?"

As soon as Maria had gone Enid turned to Elizabeth. "So what was that you were saying about no one being dumb enough to believe that you and Kris were a couple?"

"I'm going to talk to him," said Elizabeth. "I am definitely going to talk to him."

Enid's eyebrow went up. "Today?"

Elizabeth frowned. "Tomorrow."

"What's wrong with today?" Enid persisted.

"It's too soon," said Elizabeth. "I need time to work out what I'll say. I'll tell him at the party. It's the perfect opportunity."

* * *

Sam was late. Jessica, looking even prettier than usual in a green print sundress, sat on the sofa, one eye out the window and one eye on the clock on the mantel. "You'd better have a good excuse that doesn't involve your dirt bike, Sam," she muttered.

Mrs. Wakefield came into the room. "You still here?" she asked. "Elizabeth and Kris left long ago."

Jessica sighed. "If I know Sam, he suddenly decided to adjust a couple of valves or something at the last minute and he's forgotten the time."

But her mother wasn't interested in Sam. "Kris seems like a very nice boy," she said lightly.

"Yeah," Jessica agreed, "he's OK."

"Very different from Todd, though," Mrs. Wakefield continued.

"Um," said Jessica, "I guess so."

Mrs. Wakefield fiddled with the vase of flowers on the end table for a moment or two. Then she said, "I'm a little surprised that Elizabeth's going out with him. He doesn't really seem like her type."

It's too bad he doesn't know that, Jessica thought. But to her mother she said, "Oh, really?"

Mrs. Wakefield gave her an amused smile. "Yes," she said. "Really. Don't you think so?"

Jessica wished her mother wouldn't ask her direct questions. It was so hard to squirm out of them, especially when Mrs. Wakefield looked at her like that. She knew that if she started talking, she would wind up saying too much, and then Elizabeth would be mad at her because she could never keep a secret.

"I'm not saying I don't like him," Mrs. Wakefield said. "He just seems a little . . . um . . . intense for your sister."

Miraculously, just at that moment the doorbell rang. Jessica nearly collapsed with relief. "There's Sam, Mom," she said. "I have to go."

It didn't take Elizabeth long to realize that, as far as perfect opportunities went, Maria's party was a minus five on a scale of one to ten. It was crowded, it was noisy, and it was filled with people who wanted to keep Elizabeth and Kris from being alone. Every time she managed to get him into a corner where she didn't actually have to scream to be heard, someone would join them or dance between them.

"This is some party, isn't it?" asked Kris.

"Well, it certainly looks as though everyone came." Elizabeth smiled.

He nodded, stepping out of the way of a couple who were trying to get to the refreshments. "I'm not really much of a party person," he admitted. "I don't like crowds." Two other people returning from the food table shoved past him, pushing him into Elizabeth's arms. "On the other hand," he said, looking into her eyes, "there are some good things to be said for crowds."

Elizabeth blushed. *Now,* she urged herself. *You have to tell him now.* "Well, I suppose so," she said, trying to step back but finding herself against the wall. "But at the moment I'd really like to be alone with you."

The way his blue eyes lit up made her heart

sink. Maybe this was going to be harder than she had thought. Maybe she should have paid more attention to her sister when she had tried to warn her that Kris really had a crush on her.

"I always want to be alone with you," he said, moving so close that for a second she thought he was going to kiss her.

Elizabeth took a deep breath. "No," she started to explain, "I don't mean that the way you think—" Someone turned the stereo up and Elizabeth's words were drowned out by the sound made by three guitars, an electric organ, and a drum kit. "Talk!" Elizabeth shouted.

Kris laughed, gesturing that he couldn't hear her. The smell of aftershave engulfed her as he moved closer again.

"Come on!" screamed Elizabeth, grabbing his hand. "Follow me!"

She led Kris to Mr. Santelli's study. Full of resolve and determination, she opened the door and stepped into the room. And then she froze in place. On the sofa, sitting close together in one corner, were Todd and Peggy. Todd had his arm about the back of the couch and was leaning so close to Peggy that Elizabeth knew she must have almost caught them in a kiss. Her heart started to race. Todd was telling Peggy he loved her! That was what was happening. He had only broken up with her a few weeks before, and already he was telling someone *else* he loved her! She forced her voice to work. "Oops!" she said brightly, wondering if they would be able to hear her over the racket her heart was making. "Wrong room." And then she turned around so quickly that she stepped on Kris's foot. Pushing him aside, she ran past him.

But he grabbed hold of her and pulled her over to the staircase. "Hey," he said gently, putting his arm around her. "Don't get so upset. We don't need a room. We can be alone right here."

Elizabeth was fighting so hard to keep herself from crying that Kris's lips were on hers before she knew what was happening. Somehow the warmth of his kisses made her forget the scene in the study, and she found herself responding to him. *Just because Todd doesn't find me attractive anymore doesn't mean that no one does,* she told herself.

"I can't tell you how long I've been waiting for this," Kris whispered. "I've been counting the days." He pulled her down on the stairs, and his kissing took on a new urgency.

Alarm bells went off in Elizabeth's head. What was she doing? Not only was she making a public spectacle of herself, something she had never done before, but she was using this boy to get back at Todd. "Stop it!" she ordered, pushing him away. "Stop it! I want to get out of here." She got to her feet.

"What's wrong?" he asked. "I thought you—"

"Kris, please," Elizabeth pleaded. "Let's go now!"

Silently, they walked out to the car. Silently, they got into the car. He started the engine and pulled into the road. Kris was the first to speak. "Why don't we drive up to Miller's Point?" he asked.

Elizabeth turned to him in disbelief. She had assumed that he understood what had upset her, but obviously he didn't. Miller's Point was the favorite "parking" spot for Sweet Valley High students. "I don't want to go to Miller's Point, Kris," said Elizabeth, her voice gentle but firm. "I want to go home."

There was disbelief in his look as well. "Home?" he asked. And then he smiled. "Oh, I get it," he said with a short laugh. "Your parents are out, and we'll have the house to ourselves."

"No, Kris," said Elizabeth, staring straight ahead at the oncoming traffic. "You don't understand," she said. "I want to go home. And I don't want to go out with you anymore."

"Oh, sure." He grinned. "You drag me out of the party to make out and then you decide that you don't want to see me anymore."

The headlights coming toward them were blurring. Elizabeth took a deep breath. "No," she insisted, "I didn't want to make out with you. I wanted to tell you that I wasn't going to see you anymore."

Elizabeth was used to Todd's even temper and reasonableness. Which meant that she was totally unprepared for Kris's reaction.

"What are you talking about?" he demanded. *"You don't want to go out with me anymore?"* And then he started screaming and shouting. She had never seen anyone so angry before. He accused her of leading him on. Of trying to make a fool out of him. He started shaking his fist in the air.

"Pull over!" Elizabeth ordered. "Pull over right now!" She was still several blocks from home, but there was no way she was going another yard with him in that state.

Slightly to her surprise, he pulled over.

Elizabeth unsnapped her seatbelt, picked up her bag, and opened the door.

He took hold of her arm. "You're just teasing me, aren't you?" he asked, suddenly calm again. "That's it, isn't it? You're just teasing me. You couldn't have kissed me like that if you didn't like me. You weren't pretending. That was for real."

All at once he was trying to kiss her again.

"Let me go!" she shouted, pushing him away.

"No," he said. "I don't believe you. You want to go out with me, I know you do."

"Stop it!" she screamed. "I mean it, Kris, leave me alone!" Elizabeth grabbed hold of the door and pulled in one direction as Kris pulled in the other. In the struggle, her bag fell out of her hand, and its contents spilled all over the floor of the car. "Now look what you've done," she whispered, fighting back the tears again.

Suddenly he seemed to realize that he had gone too far. "I'm sorry, Elizabeth," he said, "I really am. Let me help you—"

"Don't help me," she yelled at him, scooping everything up as quickly as she could. "I don't want your help. I just want to go home."

Angry again, he threw the car into gear. "Suit yourself," he said, and started to move off even before she had shut the door.

Jessica had seen her sister bolt from the party. She was so concerned that she asked Sam to take her home early.

"Jessica Wakefield's leaving a party early?" kidded Sam. "You really must be worried."

Jessica knew that he was trying to make her feel better. "Oh, you know what they say," she joked back. "Blood is thicker than diet cola."

Elizabeth was still up when Jessica got home. Not only was she still up, but she was pulling her room apart.

"What's going on?" Jessica asked, noticing the traces of tears on her sister's cheeks but deciding to ignore them. "Don't tell me you've misplaced something."

Elizabeth sat down on the bed. "I can't find my journal," she said, her voice shaking slightly. "I've looked all over for it."

Jessica sat down beside her. "Well, let's be logical. Where did you put it after you wrote in it last night?"

"I didn't," said Elizabeth. "I got back from Enid's really late, and I was so tired that I went straight to bed."

Jessica put her arm around her sister's shoulders. "I wouldn't worry, Liz," she told her. "You're always losing track of it lately. You probably left it in your locker or in *The Oracle* office. That's happened before."

"You're right," said Elizabeth, a little of the tension leaving her voice. She leaned on Jessica's shoulder. "I've had such an awful night that I guess I just overreacted."

"What happened? Did you talk to Kris?"

Elizabeth told her twin about finding Todd and Peggy in Mr. Santelli's study, and about the horrible scene in Kris's car. "I guess you were right," she finished. "He *was* pretty serious about me."

Jessica hugged her again. "Well, at least it's over," she comforted.

Tears welled up in Elizabeth's eyes. "Everything's over," she snuffled. "Todd *and* Kris. Everything." She took the tissue Jessica handed her. "Oh, I wish I had my journal," she whispered. "I really could use it tonight."

Ten

Elizabeth went straight to her locker when she arrived at school on Monday morning. "Please let it be there," she whispered as she unlocked the door. But just as she pulled it open, Kris slipped in front of her. Elizabeth was so surprised to see him that it took her a few seconds to realize that he was holding out a single white rose. "What's this?" she asked.

"A peace offering," said Kris, his eyes not quite meeting hers. "I want to apologize for the other night, Liz. I don't think you realize how much I . . . I . . . well, I really went off the deep end, and I'm sorry."

Elizabeth's surprise turned to relief. All day Sunday, she had been alternately furious with Kris and guilty about him. Deep in her heart, she knew that although he had behaved badly, she had behaved badly, too, by ignoring his feelings for her and using him to get back at Todd. "I'm sorry, too," she said, "I never meant to hurt you, Kris. I—"

He cut her off. "No," he protested, "it was all my fault. I knew you had just broken up with Todd. I should have realized that you weren't ready to get serious again, especially not with someone like me, but instead I rushed you." He handed her the rose. "Say you'll forgive me."

"If you'll forgive me."

He leaned against her locker. "There's nothing to forgive," he answered.

By the time Kris left her, Elizabeth was not only feeling very friendly toward him, but also she had almost forgotten what she had been doing when he interrupted her. It wasn't until she reached into the locker for the books she would need for her morning classes that she remembered her journal. But it wasn't on the shelf. *I don't believe this,* she said to herself. *If it's not here, where can it be?* Standing on tiptoe, she reached to the back of the shelf, but there was nothing there. And then she saw it, jammed beneath her sneakers on the locker floor. "Now how did that get there?" she asked out loud. She shook her head. She must have been in more of a state on Friday than she had realized. She picked up the journal and tucked it into her bag.

"I guess it was pretty decent of him to apologize," said Enid when Elizabeth had recounted the latest installment of the Kris Lynch saga. "After what happened at Maria's party, I didn't think he'd be too pleasant the next time you saw him."

"Neither did I!" Elizabeth grimaced. "He was so mad Saturday that I thought he'd never even look at me again, let alone say he was sorry."

"Maybe now things can finally get back to normal," Enid said hopefully.

Elizabeth made a face. "There's nothing normal about the fact that my boyfriend is going out with a girl who laughs like a farm animal."

"You're right," Enid agreed. "Maybe instead you and I will become old maids together, going through the years with our unrequited loves. . . ."

"You still miss Hugh, don't you?" asked Elizabeth. "Even though you never want to see or speak to him again as long as you live."

Enid nodded. "Yeah," she said glumly. "I guess it's just something I have to get used to."

Elizabeth reached over and helped herself to a couple of Enid's fries. "Are you still bumping into him wherever you go?"

"No, thank goodness." Enid shrugged. "I don't know if it was just a coincidence that he seemed to be everywhere I was, or if the fact that I ran as fast as I could in the opposite direction whenever I saw him discouraged him, but he seems to be staying closer to home." She pushed back her chair and got to her feet. "Well, I've got to return some books to the library before my next class. I'll see you later, Liz."

Elizabeth bit into a fry. "Back to normal," she said with a sigh.

"Yeah," said Enid as she turned to go. "Back to normal."

Elizabeth sat by herself for several minutes, deep in thought. So much had happened in the past couple of weeks that she wondered if she even knew what normal was. How was it possible for everything to seem so right one day and so wrong the next?

"Hi, Liz," said a voice beside her.

Elizabeth jumped. She had been so involved in her thoughts that she hadn't realized she wasn't alone. But there, looking shy and faintly embarrassed, was Todd.

"I'm sorry," he said quickly, his eyes darting from her to the table to some point over her head. "I didn't mean to sneak up on you. It's just that . . . well, I was wondering if maybe we could meet after school." His eyes went to her juice container. "I really need to talk to you."

Elizabeth could feel normalcy moving farther and farther away. Just about the last thing she wanted right then was to talk to Todd. Look what had happened the last time they had had a serious conversation! She was about to give him a snappy reply, but then his eyes met hers, and she remembered exactly how much she had been missing him. If there was any chance of keeping him as a friend, she was going to have to find a new way to relate to him. "Sure," said Elizabeth. "I'll meet you at *The Oracle* office. We can talk there."

Things weren't normal yet, she decided as she

hurried to her next class, but at least they were getting better.

"So where's Elizabeth?" asked Caroline Pearce as she climbed into the Fiat beside Jessica. "Does she have a hot date with the enigmatic Kris Lynch this afternoon?"

Jessica slammed her door shut. "No," she answered coolly, "she had something to do for *The Oracle*." She pulled out of the parking space. "And anyway," she continued, deciding to make good use of Caroline's abilities as a gossip, "Liz and Kris aren't seeing each other anymore."

Caroline raised one perfectly shaped eyebrow. "That's not the way I heard it," she said.

"I just told you that she's not seeing him anymore, and I think *I* should know," replied Jessica, her voice going from cool to icy.

Caroline tossed her hair over her shoulder. "Well, presumably *he* knows whether they're seeing each other or not," she said smoothly. "And I have it from some very reliable sources that the reason Kris and Elizabeth left the party in such a hurry the other night was because they couldn't wait to get up to Miller's Point."

"Miller's Point!" Jessica hooted, making herself keep her eyes on the road. "You've got to be kidding. *My* sister did not go to Miller's Point with Kris Lynch! Have you lost your mind?"

"I'm not only saying that she went there with him," said Caroline, "I'm saying that she had a pretty wild time."

"Caroline!" Jessica couldn't believe what she was hearing. "You know Elizabeth. You can't possibly believe what you're saying."

"A lot of people saw her kissing Kris at Maria's party," Caroline pointed out. "That wasn't typical Elizabeth Wakefield behavior, either. And the person who told me all this is none other than Kris Lynch's best friend's girlfriend. So, yes, I can possibly believe what I'm saying."

Jessica's blue-green eyes flashed. "I don't care who saw them kissing at the party," she snapped. "A quick kiss in public isn't exactly the same thing as a wild night at Miller's Point."

"It wasn't so quick," said Caroline. "And Alison Starr isn't the sort of person who makes things up. If she says she knows they went to Miller's Point, then they did."

"Well, someone's making it up," Jessica said. She turned sharply onto Calico Drive. "And to tell you the truth, I'm absolutely amazed that you would believe such nonsense. Never mind the fact that you would believe someone you hardly know over *me*!"

"I know it seems kind of farfetched, but I'm telling you, Alison was absolutely positive. She couldn't have been surer if she had pictures."

Jessica's cheeks burned with anger. "I don't know how this whole ridiculous story got started, but I'm telling you now that it's not true!"

"OK, OK," said Caroline as the Fiat jolted to a stop in front of her house. "If you're that adamant about it, I believe you." She climbed out of the car, shaking her head. "Of course I believe you.

I mean, Elizabeth? I guess someone must have gotten their wires crossed."

"Just make sure you straighten them out," snapped Jessica as she drove away.

She was feeling a little calmer as she pulled into the Wakefields' driveway. She walked into the house just as the telephone began to ring.

"Why didn't you tell me?" squealed Lila as soon as Jessica picked up the phone. "I don't believe I had to hear it from someone else."

"Tell you what?" Jessica asked.

"Oh, don't play games with me," Lila ordered. "It's all over school about Elizabeth and Kris Lynch and their night of passion at Miller's Point."

"What?" Jessica gasped. "Lila, what are you talking about?"

But Lila was too excited to be bothered with details. "And I used to think that Elizabeth was a cold fish!" She laughed.

Jessica's expression became grim. "When I find out the source of these rumors, they're going to be a *dead* fish," she said.

Todd was waiting for Elizabeth outside *The Oracle* office. She marched down the hallway toward him, determined to be calm and unemotional. She had Kris's white rose tucked into her notebook. *I will not let him see me upset,* she told herself. *I will not behave like a child.*

And then he smiled that old familiar smile. "Hi, Liz," he said.

"Look, Todd," she said as she hurried them

inside, "I think I know what you want to talk about." She began rearranging the papers on her desk. As long as she didn't look at him, she would be all right.

"You do?"

She nodded. "Yes, and I want you to know that I . . . that you and . . ." What was wrong with her? Why couldn't she finish one simple sentence? Elizabeth leaned on the desk to stop her hands from shaking. "That I'm glad you told me yourself."

He stood behind her. "Told you what?"

"About you and Peggy."

"But Elizabeth," said Todd, "I haven't told you anything yet."

"You don't have to. As soon as I saw you two in Mr. Santelli's study the other night, I guessed what was happening."

Gently, he put his hands on her shoulders and turned her toward him. "You guessed that I was telling Peggy I couldn't see her anymore because of how I feel about you? That I've been such a fool that I almost threw away the best part of my life?"

Slowly, she raised her eyes to his. "What?" she whispered.

"I've been a real jerk, Liz," said Todd. "I don't know what got into me. I guess the whole thing with Steven and Cara upset me more than I realized." He smiled ruefully. "And then Peggy started flirting with me and, well, I guess I just had to find out if you and I were together because we really cared for each other, or just because we were so comfortable together."

Elizabeth felt as though she were just waking up from an awful dream. "You weren't telling Peggy you loved her?"

He shook his head. "Of course not. As soon as we started going out I knew we weren't right for each other, but Peggy really seemed to like me, and I just found myself going along with it. But when I saw you at the party with Kris, I realized I had to break things off with Peggy. I knew I still loved you."

"Oh, Todd, I was sure you didn't care about me anymore!"

"I had the right idea, Liz, but I went about it the wrong way." He took her hand in his. "But I did find out that the reason we're together is because you're the only girl I want to be with."

All of the unhappiness and worry she had been feeling evaporated into the air. "Me, too," said Elizabeth, smiling and crying at the same time. "I've missed you so much."

He squeezed her hand. "I wouldn't blame you if you told me to get lost, but I'd prefer it if you'd give me another chance."

"I declare our trial separation a complete failure," said Elizabeth, throwing her arms around him.

"Let's go to the Box Tree Café tomorrow night to celebrate," whispered Todd. "I want the whole world to see that we're back together."

Elizabeth hugged him tightly. "Only if you'll take a walk along the beach with me now."

* * *

Jessica spent the afternoon pacing back and forth in the living room, waiting for Elizabeth to come home. By the time Elizabeth did return, floating into the house with a big grin on her face, Jessica was beside herself.

She grabbed her sister's hand and started dragging her up the stairs. "Come on!" she hissed. "Mom's in the kitchen. We have to talk!"

"Aren't you going to ask me where I've been?" asked Elizabeth. "Didn't you notice who drove me home?"

But Jessica didn't care where Elizabeth had been, and she had too much on her mind to have noticed whose car she had climbed out of. "Not now, Liz. I think something weird is going on." Jessica opened the door to her room and pulled Elizabeth in.

Elizabeth threw herself on the bed. "I've been with Todd!" she announced. "We're back together! Isn't that great?"

Jessica sat down beside her twin. "I'm really happy for you, Liz, but you've got to listen to me. Caroline and Lila—"

Elizabeth waved her hand dismissively. "You know what I think of Caroline and Lila and their stories," she said. "I really don't want to hear it."

"But it's about you," Jessica insisted. "Someone's spreading the rumor that you and Kris went up to Miller's Point Saturday night and had a pretty wild time."

Jessica had expected this information to infuriate Elizabeth the way it had infuriated her, but instead her sister laughed. Jessica stared at her in amazement. How could she laugh about something like this?

"That's ridiculous," scoffed Elizabeth. "Kris apologized to me first thing this morning." She flopped back on a pile of clothes. "And besides, anybody who knows me knows that it isn't true. If you ask me, Caroline and Lila are just stirring things up."

Jessica shook her head. "They're not like that," she protested. "They may like to gossip, but they're not malicious."

Elizabeth looked over at her. "They're not?"

Jessica sighed. "Well, they're not *that* malicious."

"I can't believe that you, of all people, are taking this so seriously," said Elizabeth. She propped herself on one elbow and smiled at her sister. "You'll see," she assured her. "By tomorrow they'll be talking about somebody else."

Eleven

When Enid strode into the girls' bathroom on Tuesday morning, there were two sophomores she didn't know combing their hair at the mirrors. Enid joined them, peering carefully at herself in the glass, fixing her hair with her fingers.

The door opened and Jean West came in. "Enid!" she cried. "You're just the person I've been looking for. Maybe you can put an end to these stupid rumors."

Enid looked at her curiously. "What stupid rumors?" she demanded.

"You mean you haven't heard them?" asked Jean. With an uneasy glance at the sophomores, she lowered her voice. "Everybody's saying that Elizabeth made Kris Lynch take her up to Miller's Point Saturday night, and that she really got carried away."

Enid stared at Jean in disbelief. "That's the biggest lie I've ever heard!" she shouted. The two sophomores turned to look at them, but Enid didn't care who heard her. "I happen to know for a fact that Elizabeth left the party early in order to break off with Kris."

"Well, that's not what he says," Jean informed her.

"Well, it's what I say," Enid roared. "And she's my best friend!"

Todd was whistling to himself as he climbed into his BMW after school when a high female voice interrupted his thoughts. "Todd! Wait up!"

Todd turned. Running across the parking lot toward him was Peggy Abbot herself. Considering that the last conversation they'd had had ended with her throwing a book at him and vowing that she would never speak to him again, Todd was a little surprised that she seemed so eager to talk to him now.

"Hi, Peggy," he said cautiously.

Peggy skidded to a stop. Her cheeks were pink, and she was out of breath. She got straight to the point. "Todd," she said, "have you heard the rumors about Elizabeth that are going around?"

"Rumors?" asked Todd. "What rumors?"

Peggy immediately launched into an account of what she had heard.

When she was done, Todd started to laugh. "I know you're mad at me, Peggy," he said good-naturedly, "but if you think I'd believe anything like that about Elizabeth for even a second, you're very mistaken."

"I'm not telling you this because I'm mad at

you," said Peggy. "And I'm not making it up, either." She leaned down toward him earnestly. "It's all over the school, Todd. I've heard it from at least four different people, including Kris himself. According to him, he practically had to fight her off."

Todd's smile vanished. "You heard *Kris* telling this story?"

Peggy nodded. "Not five minutes ago. I was sitting outside at one of the tables, and I overheard him talking to his friends."

Todd got out of the car so quickly that Peggy had to jump back to get out of his way. He slammed the door shut. "I think I'd better go have a talk with Mr. Lynch. There's no way I'm going to let him get away with spreading these lies."

Todd found Kris sitting by himself on the lawn, doodling in a sketchpad. "I'd like to have a word with you, Lynch," said Todd, coming to a stop in front of him.

Kris looked up with a bored expression on his face. "Yeah?"

"Yeah. I want you to know that I heard all about what happened between you and Elizabeth Saturday night, and I want you to stop spreading these lies about her, as of yesterday."

No flicker of emotion showed on Kris's face. "Are you threatening me?"

"I'm not threatening you," said Todd, "I'm telling you."

A humorless smile spread across Kris's face. "And what if they're not lies?" he wanted to know. "What if everything I've been saying is true?"

Todd couldn't hide his contempt. "Who are you kidding? Anybody who knows Elizabeth knows that there hasn't been one word of truth in anything you've said."

"Really?" Kris's smile became broader. "Well, maybe you don't know Elizabeth as well as you think you do. With me, she's her real self. She doesn't hide anything." He held up two crossed fingers. "We're very close, me and Liz. So close that I know things about you you think nobody knows."

"Oh, sure you do," Todd sneered.

"You don't believe me?" The smile froze. While Todd stood rooted to the ground, stunned into silence, Kris listed some of the most intimate details of Todd's relationship with Elizabeth. He knew about their arguments. He knew about their secrets. He even knew about their most romantic times together. The more Kris talked, the more Todd's world seemed to be crashing down around him. How could Elizabeth betray him like this?

"She's only pretending to get back together with you, you know." Kris laughed. "To pay you back for running around with Peggy. Didn't you see her carrying that rose I gave her yesterday? I'm the one she really loves."

Ten minutes earlier, Todd had been the happiest person in the world. Now he was the most miserable. Without another word, Todd turned away. Kris's laughter followed him across the grass.

* * *

Enid had told Elizabeth at lunch about her encounter with Jean West. She had expected Elizabeth to be as outraged as she was, but instead Elizabeth was so happy about getting back together with Todd that she had dismissed it all as idle gossip.

"You'll see," she had reassured Enid, "no one really believes any of this nonsense."

But Enid *was* worried. Even people who knew Elizabeth seemed to believe the stories that were circulating about Elizabeth and Kris.

What sort of a person would tell such awful lies? Enid wondered as she walked down Main Street after school.

Enid stopped so suddenly that the woman behind her walked into her. There, just coming out of the deli, was Kris Lynch himself, carrying a bright yellow plastic bag. He turned to the right and started toward her.

Enid half expected that Kris, knowing she was Elizabeth's best friend, would try to avoid her, but instead he gave her a big smile. "Hi, Enid," he greeted her. "How are you doing?"

"You have some nerve, you creep," she snapped back. "How can you smile at me after spreading all those disgusting rumors about Elizabeth?"

The smile didn't falter. "I don't know what you're talking about, Enid," said Kris. "I haven't spread any rumors about Elizabeth. All I've done is tell the truth."

Enid could feel her temper rising. "The truth?"

she shouted. "The truth is that Elizabeth has too much taste to go out with someone like you."

For just a second the smile slipped, but he recovered almost instantly. "Is that what she said?" he asked. He shook his head. "I'm surprised at how little Elizabeth's told you about our relationship, since you *are* her best friend." He winked. "She's certainly told me all about you."

Enid frowned, wondering what he was getting at. "What do you mean?" she asked.

"You know, Enid," he said, "all about how badly you wanted to get back together with Hugh."

Enid felt as though she had been knifed in the back. "How do you know that?" she hissed, too thunderstruck to deny what he was saying.

His laughter echoed down the street. "I thought it was hilarious the way you made up the story about the lost earring, and then Hugh actually found it!" He shook his head. "But I think you should have given him a chance to explain about the girl in the bike shop, Enid. I mean, it *is* possible that you jumped to the wrong conclusion."

Part of Enid wanted to hit him over the head with her shoulder bag; the other half wanted to burst into tears. How could Elizabeth do this to her? All the while she had been pretending to be Enid's friend, she had been laughing about her with a jerk like this and telling him her secrets!

"Hey, Enid!" Kris called after her. "Don't go away. We have a lot more to talk about!"

* * *

Elizabeth, dressed in a sea-green dress, her hair pulled back with matching ribbons, spun around in the middle of the kitchen. "Well?" she asked, facing her family again. "How do I look?"

"Terrific," said Mr. Wakefield.

"You look lovely, dear," said her mother.

Jessica smiled. "You look great."

Elizabeth couldn't sit still, she was so excited about her date with Todd. She had spent the entire afternoon after school getting ready for it, and now she didn't know what to do with herself.

"Big date?" asked Mrs. Wakefield.

Elizabeth nodded. "Todd should be here any minute," she said. "He's taking me to the Box Tree Café for dinner."

Mr. Wakefield held a forkful of spaghetti in the air. "Where has he been lately?" he asked with a faintly puzzled air. "I haven't seen him around."

"Well, from now on you're going to see a lot of him," Elizabeth answered happily. She sat down at her place and helped herself to a glass of juice while the rest of the family continued with their meal.

"You know," said Jessica, "I was reading this really fascinating article about Jeeps the other day . . ."

Jessica droned on about Jeeps and their reliability and usefulness while Elizabeth lost herself in imagining what her evening was going to be like. Eventually she became aware that her father and sister were clearing the table. She looked at the clock. Todd was thirty minutes late.

Mrs. Wakefield put the dessert on the table and Jessica started talking about the new safety features on four-wheel-drive vehicles. The next time Elizabeth looked at the clock, Todd was fifty minutes late.

Jessica got to her feet. "I don't have to meet Sam for another half-hour," she explained to no one in particular, "but I figure I should give myself some extra time in case the car breaks down again."

"That's very sensible," said Mr. Wakefield with a knowing smile.

Her parents went out for a walk, and Elizabeth went into the living room to wait for Todd. She looked at her watch. If he didn't turn up soon, they would be going out for breakfast. She pulled back the curtain and looked out the window. Something must have happened, she decided. Maybe his car had broken down.

Elizabeth dialed Todd's number. To her surprise, he answered on the second ring.

"I figured it would be you," he said sharply.

Thinking he was joking, Elizabeth laughed. "Well, of course it's me. I'm all dressed up with nowhere to go. Have you lost track of the time? You were supposed to pick me up over an hour ago."

"I thought you'd rather go out with Kris Lynch tonight than with me," said Todd coldly. "Considering how close the two of you have become." He slammed down the phone.

Elizabeth stared at the receiver as though it had bitten her. "This can't be happening," she said out loud, her blue-green eyes filling with tears. "Todd can't believe those stupid rumors."

Her head swimming, Elizabeth automatically dialed Enid's number next. "I should have listened to you and Jessica," Elizabeth started saying as soon as Enid picked up the phone. "You warned me about those stories that are going around school, and now it turns out that Todd believes them, too!" She choked back a sob. "Can you believe that, Enid? Todd thinks the things they're saying about me are true."

"Yes," said Enid, her voice as friendly as a polar bear. "I can believe that."

For the second time in five minutes, Elizabeth was left staring at a dead receiver.

Jessica had complained so much about the Fiat's unreliability that Sam had insisted on following her home. "What if it did break down on the way home?" he had asked. "It happened to Enid, didn't it?" And then he had given her an evil smile. "If you're going to break down on some dark and lonely street, I want to be with you," he had whispered.

Jessica pulled into the driveway, and Sam pulled in after her. "I wonder if Liz has come home from her big date with Todd yet," she said as he walked her to the door.

Sam laughed. "Are you kidding? They probably haven't even started dessert yet. If I hadn't been out with you for over three weeks, I probably wouldn't have looked at the *menu* yet."

Jessica leaned against his shoulder. "I never thought I'd say this," she whispered, "but I'm so relieved they got back together. Elizabeth was miserable without him."

"I just hope she's right about this gossip," said Sam. "From what you said, it sounds like this Lynch guy is out to get her."

Jessica shrugged. "I was really worried yesterday," she admitted. "But now that Todd's back on the scene, I'm sure everything will be all right."

Jessica watched Sam drive off, then she let herself into the house. She went upstairs and into her room. Then, deciding to see if Elizabeth was home after all, she walked through the bathroom to her sister's room.

Elizabeth was asleep on her bed, her journal open beside her and her dress thrown in a heap on the floor. The uneasy feeling grew. That wasn't like Elizabeth, to just drop her clothes on the rug like that and fall asleep with the light still on.

Jessica went over and pulled the covers around her sister. As she picked up the journal to put it away she glanced at the last entry. Horror-stricken, she read what had happened that evening. The last line Elizabeth had written went straight to her heart. *What hurts most is that Todd and Enid, two of the people I love most in the world, have turned against me. Why? I've never knowingly done anything to hurt either of them.*

Deep in thought, Jessica closed the journal and put it on Elizabeth's dresser. Then she turned off the light and tiptoed back to her own room.

But a half-hour later, she was still wide awake, looking out the window at the starry night. Something was very wrong, but Jessica couldn't quite figure out what it was. All she was certain of was that neither Todd nor Enid would believe Kris's lies about Elizabeth if that was all there was to it. They knew Elizabeth too well. There had to be something more; something else must have happened that Jessica didn't know about. With a sigh, she pulled the curtain closed. *Well, there's only one thing to do,* she thought as she climbed into bed. *And that's find out what that something else is.*

Twelve

It was Wednesday morning, and Elizabeth felt terrible. Everything looked the same at Sweet Valley High, but everything was different. Her best friends wouldn't talk to her, and everyone else was talking about her.

Elizabeth could feel people watching her as she walked past, and she could hear their giggles and whispers. *Don't let them get to you,* she told herself. *Just keep your eyes straight and act like everything is normal.* Determined, she went straight to Enid's locker, as she did every other morning.

Enid was getting her books out as Elizabeth came up behind her. "Enid," she said tentatively, "I don't know why you're so mad at me, but I'm sure if we could just talk—"

Enid turned around slowly, a contemptuous look on her face. "Oh, you know all right," she answered in a heavy whisper. "You know exactly why." She slammed her locker shut. "I just can't believe that you have the nerve to speak to me after what you've done," Enid continued, her eyes burning with rage.

"But, Enid, you at least owe me—"

"Nothing!" Enid's voice rose above the noise in the hall. "I don't owe you anything, Elizabeth Wakefield. Do you hear me? Nothing at all!"

"Enid, if you'd just calm down—"

"Nothing," raged Enid. *"N-o-t-h-i-n-g!"* She spun on her heel and stormed away.

Her face burning, Elizabeth glanced around to see if anyone had witnessed her humiliation. No one was looking at her. She took a deep breath. *It's OK,* she told herself. *Just act like nothing happened.*

The next thing that didn't happen that morning was that Todd, seeing her from the other end of the hallway, immediately did an about-face and went back the other way. *It's all right,* Elizabeth told herself again, *you're just having some weird dream and in a little while you'll wake up.*

But the day dragged on, and Elizabeth didn't wake up. She walked from class to class by herself. She ate lunch alone in the newspaper office. The only people who behaved normally with her were Jessica, who, when she saw her, linked arms and chatted in her usual bubbly way, and Kris. Although Elizabeth wasn't so sure that Kris's behavior could be called normal. Every time he saw her, he gave her a big smile and what seemed to be a meaningful wink. "I wish I still had his rose," Elizabeth said to Jessica as they watched him disappear around a corner. "I'd like to shove it down his throat."

Jessica smiled sweetly. "Why stop at one rose?" she asked. "Why not the whole thorny bouquet?"

Jessica knew exactly how much pain Elizabeth was in. Even if she had not read that last entry in Elizabeth's journal the night before, she would have known from the expression in her sister's eyes. Elizabeth's brave smile didn't fool her twin. Elizabeth couldn't believe what was happening to her, but at the same time she felt powerless to stop it. Jessica, however, was not powerless. She was angry. She was also stubborn, determined, and not about to act as though nothing was happening when something strange was going on. Elizabeth wasn't going to suffer for one second longer than necessary, not if she had anything to say about it.

"Mind if I join you?" asked Jessica brightly.

Enid, reading while she ate her lunch, looked up in surprise. "Well, as a matter of fact, I do," she protested, but Jessica was already putting her tray on the table and pulling out a chair.

"Thanks." She sat down and looked straight into Enid's eyes. "I'm not going to beat around the bush," she informed her. "I know that you and Elizabeth have had some sort of falling-out, and I'd like to know why."

Enid glared back at her. "Why don't you ask her?"

"Because she doesn't know. She has absolutely no idea why you're mad at her."

"Oh, she knows all right," snapped Enid. "You don't go around blabbing people's personal secrets to strangers and not know it."

Jessica leaned forward, trying to make sense out of what she was hearing. "Are you saying that Elizabeth told *your* secrets to someone else?"

Enid nodded. "Yes," she said, "that's exactly what I'm saying."

"But that's impossible. Elizabeth wouldn't even tell *me* something you'd told her in confidence," Jessica reasoned.

"Well, she did. She was sworn to secrecy, but that didn't stop her."

"I don't believe it," she said, shaking her head. "Who did she tell?"

Enid smiled smugly. "Kris Lynch."

"Kris Lynch?" The idea that Elizabeth would confide anything in Kris was beyond ridiculous. "Enid," she gasped, "you've got to be joking. Elizabeth hardly knows him!"

"Well, that's not what he says," said Enid. "He claims that they're *very* close." She proceeded to recount her conversation with him the previous afternoon. "You can imagine how stunned I was," said Enid when she had finished. "There I was, standing in the middle of Main Street in broad daylight, and he was telling me things about myself that no one but Elizabeth knew."

"I admit it looks bad," Jessica said slowly, "but you *know* Elizabeth would never betray your secrets to anyone else. She's the most trustworthy person I've ever known."

Enid's voice wobbled with emotion. "I know that," she said. "I thought about it all night long. But, Jessica, he *knows* all of those things about me. And unless he's psychic, the only way he could have found out was from Liz."

* * *

"Look, Jessica," said Todd, "I know how close you and Elizabeth are, but I really don't want to talk about this with you."

Jessica had followed Todd to his locker after lunch, resolved to make him talk to her. Todd, however, was even more unwilling to discuss what had happened than Enid had been.

Jessica folded her arms across her chest. "But I want to talk about it with you," she said calmly. "After all you and Liz have been through together, I think you owe her some sort of explanation for suddenly turning on her like this."

"*I* owe *her* an explanation?" Todd yanked his locker door open. "After what she's done?" He pulled some books from the shelf. "It's been delightful talking to you, Jessica," he said, banging the door shut. "But I have to go or I'll be late for class."

Jessica grabbed his arm. "Wait a minute," she begged. "Just wait one minute." She gave a quick glance around and lowered her voice. "This awful thing that Liz did—was it that she told Kris Lynch private things about you?"

Todd's jaw dropped in surprise. "How did you know that?" he asked. "Did Elizabeth—"

"Elizabeth doesn't know anything about this," Jessica cut in. "It was only a guess."

"Only a guess?" Todd looked at her with interest. "It was a pretty lucky guess. Unless, of course, you've been talking to Kris."

"Actually," said Jessica, "it was Enid I was talking to."

"Enid?"

Jessica nodded. She was beginning to feel that she was getting somewhere—if only she knew *where*. "Why don't I walk you to your class, and I'll tell you all about it?"

When she had finished telling Todd what Enid had told her, he shook his head. "It still doesn't make any sense," he said. "As hard as it is to believe that Liz would betray me or Enid, what else can I believe?"

Jessica's golden hair swung angrily. "That this creep is lying, of course!" she exclaimed.

"But he knows stuff about me and Elizabeth that he could only have heard from her, Jess. Stuff even you wouldn't know."

Jessica adjusted her books. "Then I guess it's time I *did* talk to Mr. Lynch," she said with a grim smile.

As soon as the bell rang to end her last class, Jessica was on her feet and bolting for the door. She was going to be there when Kris Lynch walked out of the building, no matter what.

As soon as he saw her Kris gave her a big, friendly smile.

Jessica took a step forward. "I'd like to talk to you for a minute," she said.

She had expected him to make some excuse or try to avoid her, but instead his eyes lit up as though he had been hoping for just this to happen. "Great," he exclaimed. "I can't think of anything I'd rather do."

Jessica Wakefield was a schemer. That was why

she immediately realized that she was in the presence of a real master. *It takes one to know one,* she said to herself as they walked to a bench on the lawn.

"So," said Kris as they sat down, "what can I do for you?"

"You can stop spreading these foul lies about my sister, that's what you can do." She gave him her sweetest smile. "Because if you don't, I'm going to have to force you to."

He stared back at her, the picture of innocence. "Me?" he asked. "But I'm not spreading any lies about your sister, Jessica. Every word out of my mouth has been the complete truth."

"Oh, sure," she said with a sarcastic nod. "And I live in a castle and keep a unicorn in the garden."

He shook his head sadly. "I'm hurt that you don't believe me. I would've thought that of all people, Elizabeth would've told *you* how close we are."

"Oh, she told me how close you are," said Jessica. "About as close as New York and San Francisco."

"A little closer than that," he said, laughing softly. "I mean, she wouldn't have told me all about you and the trouble you got into over that teen party line if we weren't close, would she?" His voice became warmer. "Or about you and that cult? Or the time you tried to turn all the cheerleaders against Claire Middleton?"

Jessica's blue-green eyes showed no emotion as she listened to Kris rattle off some of the more intimate details of her life. Unlike Todd and Enid, Jessica was neither thunderstruck nor overcome with a sense of betrayal. What she was was angry; angrier than she had ever been before. While he was still talking, she got calmly to her feet. "You listen to me, you reptile," she said in a loud, clear voice. "I don't know how you know these things, but I know my sister never told them to you." She shook an accusing finger at him. "I'm going to find out how you know them, though, you can be sure of that."

"Is that a threat?" asked Kris in mock horror.

"No." Jessica winked. "It's a promise."

Elizabeth was feeling so miserable that she had told her mother she was sick and had stayed in her room rather than join the family for dinner. Jessica, absentmindedly going through the motions of eating, wished *she* had had the sense to think of an excuse. She pushed her vegetables from one side of the plate to the other, but the last thing she felt like doing was eating. Her mind was too full of Kris Lynch and what he was up to.

"Jessica," said Mrs. Wakefield, obviously not for the first time, "would you *mind* passing me the salad?"

Jessica blinked. "Oh, sure," she said. "Sorry."

"I don't believe this." Mrs. Wakefield laughed. "We've been sitting in the same room for nearly a half-hour, and you haven't said one word about four-wheel drive."

Mrs. Wakefield looked concerned. "I hope you're not coming down with whatever your sister has."

"I'm fine, Mom," Jessica assured her. "I'm just thinking, that's all. I have sort of a problem."

Mr. Wakefield grinned. "What's his name?"

Jessica rolled her eyes. "It's nothing like that. This is a real problem. It's almost like a brain-teaser or a mystery." She moved a slice of tomato from the left side of her plate to the right. "I just can't figure it out. No matter which way I look at it, it doesn't make any sense at all."

"Well, you know what Sherlock Holmes always said, don't you?" offered Mr. Wakefield.

Jessica smiled. "No," she said, the dimple showing in her left cheek. "What did Sherlock Holmes always say?"

"That once you've eliminated the impossible, whatever's left, no matter how improbable, must be the solution."

"And you know what Alice Wakefield always says," her mother broke in, pointing at Jessica's full plate. "She who doesn't eat her salad doesn't get any double chocolate-chip ice cream for dessert."

"Once you've eliminated the impossible, whatever's left, no matter how improbable, must be the solution," Jessica repeated as she climbed the stairs to her room. She knew it was impossible that Elizabeth could have told Kris those things about Todd, Enid, and her. And she knew it was impossible that anyone else had told him, because no one else knew. *So now what?* she wondered.

She poked her head into her sister's room. Elizabeth was bent over her desk, writing furiously in her journal.

"I brought you some fruit," called Jessica. "In case you get hungry."

Elizabeth looked up. "Thanks," she said. "I guess I could use an apple."

Jessica stepped in and put two apples and a banana on her twin's dresser. "Are you feeling any better?' she asked.

Elizabeth managed a smile. "Actually, I am." She gestured toward the book in front of her. "Being able to unload all my feelings in my journal is really an incredible release. I don't know what I'd do without it. I just put down whatever thoughts come into my mind."

Jessica nodded. "Yeah, it must be a big help," she said as she turned toward the door, still thinking about the impossible versus the improbable.

Back in her own room, Jessica pushed a few things off the bed and flopped down. "Sherlock Holmes," she said, "where are you when I really need you?" She closed her eyes. *Impossible,* she thought. *Improbable.* And then she heard her sister saying, "I just put down whatever thoughts come into my mind."

"That's it!" Jessica shouted, opening her eyes and sitting bolt upright. "That's got to be it!" If Kris Lynch knew things that only Elizabeth could have told him, and if she hadn't told him, then he must have read her journal. Her face clouded. "What are you, dumb?" she asked herself. "That's impossible, completely impossible. Elizabeth would never let anybody read her journal. Not even me."

But then Jessica reconsidered. She *had* read her sister's journal. Not with her permission, of course, but she had read it. So it wasn't impossible that Kris had read it, too. It was only improbable. A slow smile began to appear on her face. And not very improbable, either, she decided. Hadn't Elizabeth's journal been missing right after Maria's party and her big fight with Kris? What if he had stolen it so that he could get back at her for turning him down?

Jessica hugged herself excitedly. "That has to be right!" she shouted. "It just has to be!"

Thirteen

The first thing Jessica did on Thursday morning was take Lila aside.

"Whew!" Lila whistled when Jessica had finished telling her her suspicions. "Just the idea of somebody reading my diary gives me the creeps. It's like someone being able to read your mind."

"It's worse," said Jessica. "If someone could read minds it would be accidental, wouldn't it? But this was deliberate. And not only that, he's using what he discovered to totally ruin Liz's life."

"The boy's slime," said Lila, briefly but succinctly. I know your sister and I aren't exactly the best of pals, Jessica, but I wouldn't want to see this happen to my worst enemy." Her pretty mouth curled in distaste. "I mean, I hide my diary in a different place every morning, just so burglars won't be able to find it."

Jessica grinned. Lila lived in one of the biggest,

most expensive houses in Sweet Valley. "I don't think anybody breaking into Fowler Crest would really be after your diary," she pointed out.

"You can never be too careful," said Lila. "If Elizabeth had been a little more cautious, none of this would ever have happened. But it *has* happened," she continued, "so the question now is, what are we going to do about it? Do you want me to spread some nasty rumors about Kris?"

Jessica gazed at Lila with open admiration. *That's why she's my best friend,* Jessica thought. "Not yet," she said. "But I want to convince him that that's what I *will* do if he doesn't admit that he's been lying about Liz and make a public apology."

Lila nodded. "Sounds good to me," she said. "Where do I fit in?"

She put an arm around Lila's shoulder. "I thought you might know where Mr. Lynch lives."

"I can do better than that." Lila laughed. "I'll take you there myself this afternoon!"

If Kris was surprised to open his door and find Jessica Wakefield standing on the porch, he didn't show it.

His eyes went from Jessica to Lila standing by her lime-green Triumph at the curb. "You two selling cookies door to door now?" he joked.

Jessica ignored him, marching past him while he was still speaking. "Thank you," she said coolly, "I will come in."

"Excuse me," said Kris, following her into the living room, "but unless you have some very good reason for being here, I think you'd better turn right around and go back the way you came."

Jessica sat down on the couch. "Oh, I have a very good reason for being here," she purred. "I'm here to keep my promise to you." She smiled angelically. "I always keep my promises."

"Is that right?" he asked, sitting across from her.

The smile on Jessica's face became a little less angelic. "You read my sister's diary," she said simply.

For just an instant the mask of bravado slipped from Kris's face, but he quickly put it back in place. "Oh, really?" he asked. "And how would *I* get ahold of your sister's diary? Are you suggesting that I broke into your house when no one was home and stole it?"

"Oh, you stole it all right," said Jessica. "But you didn't break into our house. She always carries it with her. All you had to do was take it from her bag when she wasn't looking."

A new, wary look had come into his eyes. "You can't prove a thing," he countered. "It's your word against mine."

"Is it?" Jessica smiled. She folded her hands on her lap and leaned toward him earnestly. "You see, I don't think I have to prove anything. I'm just going to fight fire with fire." Her eyes met his. "I'm sure that's something you can understand."

Kris laughed uneasily. "Fire with fire? What are you talking about?"

Jessica had rehearsed this scene in her mind all

afternoon. She stood up and started walking slowly around the room, the way detectives in the movies always did. "I'm going to tell everybody I know that you're a thief and a liar. I'm going to tell them that you can't be trusted for even a minute." She paused by the mantelpiece. "Then you'll get to see for yourself what it's like when the whole world turns against you."

His laugh was becoming a little thin. "And who's going to believe you?"

Jessica cocked her head to one side, pretending to consider his question. "Oh, everyone," she said at last. "All my friends at school. All my friends in town. All Sam's friends at Bridgewater High." She nodded toward the front of the house. "All of Lila's friends. It won't be long before everybody in southern California knows about you," she said softly. "You won't have a friend left."

"You're bluffing," said Kris. "You wouldn't do that."

"Oh yes I would." Jessica moved so close to him that they were almost touching. "And I can do all that just by telling the truth," she explained. "Think what I could do if I had to make some things up, the way you did about Liz."

Kris stared at her in silence for a few seconds. When he did speak, his voice was cracked and low. "It wasn't the way you think," he said. "I didn't deliberately take Elizabeth's diary. We had a fight after Maria's party, and she dropped it in the car."

"But you did deliberately read it. And you did deliberately spread those lies."

He rested his face in his hands. "I don't know what came over me, I really don't. I was going to bring it back the next day, but then I started thinking about how all my friends were going to laugh at me because Elizabeth had dumped me. Everybody told me I was nuts going after her, that she would never go out with me, but I'd been crazy about her for so long . . ." His voice trailed off.

"That's no excuse," said Jessica evenly.

"I know it's no excuse," he mumbled. "But it is an explanation. I just wanted to read what she'd said about me. I know it sounds stupid, but I thought that if I read one nice thing that she'd written about me, I'd feel better." He looked up, an ironic smile on his face. "Only there wasn't anything nice about me. She wrote that she thought I was a jerk and that the only reason she went out with me was to make Todd jealous."

In spite of herself, Jessica almost felt sorry for him. "But that isn't even true," she protested. "I don't know what Elizabeth wrote in her journal or why, but I know that she really liked and respected you. That's why she decided to stop seeing you, because she knew it was unfair to lead you on when she was still in love with Todd."

Kris sighed. "Well, maybe," he said. "I don't know anymore. All I know is that I just went nuts. I loved her so much, and the whole time she was making a fool out of me." He shrugged. "And that's when I got my brilliant idea."

"To turn everyone against her."

"No, I didn't intend that. Things just sort of

snowballed. I swear I never thought for one second that things would turn out the way they have."

Jessica rested a hand on his shoulder. "Well, I can help you out, if you really want me to," she said.

"Believe me," Jessica said, "my big mouth has gotten me into trouble enough times to understand how it happens."

She and Kris were on their way to the Dairi Burger, where Jessica had asked both Enid and Todd to meet her.

Kris shook his head as he pulled the Beetle into the parking lot. "Reading her diary was bad enough. Once I'd read one page, I just couldn't put it down, even though I knew it was wrong. But I can't believe I started those rumors about her . . ." He turned to Jessica with an expression of complete bewilderment. "I'd like to think that it was temporary insanity," he confessed.

Jessica gave him a sympathetic smile. The more she talked to Kris, the better she liked him. And what she had told him was true. She had gotten herself into enough bad situations with her schemes and her stories to recognize that she and Kris Lynch were not as unlike as they might appear. "Let's just hope your sanity *has* returned," she said with a chuckle.

Enid and Todd were already sitting at a table far at the back. As soon as Jessica walked over with Kris, Todd got to his feet. "What's going on?" he wanted to know.

"Sit down, Todd," Jessica ordered. Now that the worst was over, she was feeling a little annoyed with Todd and Enid. Although she understood how hurt and betrayed they had felt, she could not help thinking that they should have known better. "Kris has something to tell you two," she announced. "And I'm just dying for a chocolate milkshake."

"How can you waltz in here with *him* and start talking about chocolate milkshakes?" asked Todd.

Enid was nervously folding and unfolding her straw wrapper. "Does this have something to do with Liz?"

Kris nodded. "It has everything to do with her." He smiled sourly. "And with me and all the wrong I've done her."

"Wrong?" asked Todd. He looked from Kris to Jessica. "Maybe you'd better just start at the beginning."

By the time Kris was through with his confession, Enid and Todd were sitting rigidly in their seats in stunned silence, their sodas long forgotten.

"So there you have it," said Kris. "I've never been so ashamed of myself in my life." He turned to Jessica. "I give you my solemn word that I will never do anything like this again, so long as I live."

Todd found his voice before Enid. "Talk about betrayal!" he said. "It looks like all of us except Jessica have something to feel ashamed about. How could I ever have treated Elizabeth like that?"

"You?" gasped Enid. "After all Elizabeth's done

for me, I repay her by turning on her the first time someone puts a doubt in my mind." She put her head in her hands. "If I were Elizabeth, I'd never forgive me," she moaned.

Glancing over at Enid, Jessica drained the last inch of milkshake from her glass. *It's probably pretty lucky for you that you're not Elizabeth,* she said to herself.

Jessica was feeling pretty pleased with herself by the time she got home. Everything was going to be all right again—as long as she could keep from telling her sister the good news too soon. She didn't want to spoil the surprise Kris, Todd, and Enid were arranging, but at the same time she was so excited that she couldn't stand still. Jessica danced into the kitchen, singing under her breath.

Elizabeth was peeling potatoes at the sink. She glanced at her sister as she twirled into the room. "What are you so happy about?" she asked, managing a small smile. "Don't tell me Sam's decided to rename his dirt bike after you."

Jessica leaned against the counter, trying not to appear as joyous as she felt. "Me?" she asked innocently. "I'm sixteen, I'm blond, and I'm beautiful. Why shouldn't I be happy?"

Elizabeth made a face. "Well, I'm sixteen, blond, and beautiful, and I'm *not* happy. I might as well be a two-hundred-year-old troll living under a bridge."

Jessica grabbed her and spun her around. "That's what you think," she said laughingly. She scooped a handful of potato peelings from the sink and threw them in the air. "You never can tell what your fairy godmother has in store for you!" Still laughing, she started to dance out of the room.

"You're up to something," said Elizabeth, following her sister into the hall. "You get that glint in your eye when you're scheming."

"Scheming?" asked Jessica as she headed up the stairs. "Me?"

Elizabeth frowned thoughtfully. "I hope you're not doing anything I'm going to regret," she shouted.

Jessica's head reappeared at the top of the stairs. "Oh, come on, Liz," she said. "You know me!"

"That's what I'm worried about," said Elizabeth. "I *do* know you."

Later that night, just as Jessica was about to turn out the lights in her room, Elizabeth poked her head through the door. "Jess?" she whispered. "Are you still awake?"

Jessica propped herself on one elbow. "I'm awake. What's wrong?" She could just make out her sister's golden hair in the dark.

"Nothing," said Elizabeth. "I just . . . I just wanted to tell you how lucky I feel to have you as my sister, that's all. Through this whole mess, you've been the best friend I could ever want."

"Remember that the next time I want to borrow that blue silk shirt of yours," Jessica shot back.

"I'll do that." Elizabeth laughed. "Good night, Jessica."

Jessica watched the door shut behind her twin, a lump rising in her throat. "Good night, Liz," she called. She gave her pillow a thump, and closed her eyes. *I wonder if she meant it about the shirt,* she thought as she drifted off to sleep.

Elizabeth walked briskly toward *The Oracle* office on Friday afternoon. Jessica had said she had something to go in the paper, and Elizabeth had agreed to meet her there after school. Jessica, however, was being very mysterious about the whole thing and wouldn't tell her what it was. "Let's just say it's very special," she had said. "Like nothing you've ever printed before."

She was so immersed in her thoughts that she had almost reached the office door before she realized who was standing there with her sister. Feeling all the color drain out of her face, she automatically turned to run back the other way.

"Wait a minute, Liz!" urged Jessica, grabbing her hand. "I think you're going to want to hear this."

Elizabeth stared at her sister. What was she talking about? What could Kris, Enid, or Todd possibly say to her that she would want to hear?

Kris stepped forward. "Jessica's right, Elizabeth," he said gently. "I've come here to apologize to you for what I've done. Not only did I start all those rumors about you, but I lied to Enid and Todd."

Elizabeth looked at her friends.

Todd lowered his eyes. "And we believed

him," he said in a dejected voice. "Even though we know what sort of person you are, we believed everything Kris told us."

Enid was starting to cry. "I'm so ashamed of myself." She snuffled. "How could I have treated you like that?"

Elizabeth felt as though the room were spinning. The nightmare was over. It was really over. She squeezed her sister's hand.

Kris handed her a piece of paper. At the top was a cartoon. It was a picture of Elizabeth sitting on a chair, and beside her, kneeling, was Kris. The caption read, "Begging Forgiveness," and beneath was a full open apology. "I want you to run this in the paper," he said. "I don't expect you ever to forgive me, but I want at least to set the record straight."

"I wouldn't blame you if you never forgave me, either," said Todd. "I was a real jerk."

"Oh, Liz," sobbed Enid, "Liz, I'm so sorry. . . ."

Elizabeth brushed a tear from her own cheek. "There's nothing to forgive," she said, throwing her arms around her friends in a huge hug.

Todd kissed the top of her head. "Are you OK?" He grinned.

Elizabeth laughed, the first real laugh she had had in days. "Oh, I'm fine," she said with an enormous smile. "Let's just say it's been a tough week."

Guido's Pizza Palace was crowded and noisy on Friday night, but no one was having a better time than Elizabeth and the people sitting with her at a table in the back.

"No, really," Jessica was saying, "I read it on the entertainment page of the newspaper. My very favorite soap opera, *The Young and the Beautiful,* is looking for a pair of identical twins to do a guest appearance." She turned to the others. "Don't you think Liz and I would be perfect?"

"Jessica," Elizabeth replied, her voice full of affection, "do you think we could concentrate on one thing at a time? Right now I just want to enjoy this moment."

Todd, sitting next to her, leaned over and kissed her cheek. "Me, too," he whispered.

Elizabeth smiled, and her gaze moved around the table from one person to another. "I don't know if I've ever been this happy before," she announced.

Sam raised his soda in a toast. "To Elizabeth," he said.

"Not yet," she protested. "We have to wait for Enid."

Jessica grabbed Sam's arm and peered at his watch. "She's already twenty minutes late," she said. "I'm starving. Can't we order without her?"

Sam gave her a nudge. "Where's your sense of occasion?" he teased. "This is a solemn event."

Jessica winked impishly. "Yeah, I know that," she answered, "but as far as I'm concerned, it's also a pepperoni-pizza-with-double-cheese event."

Elizabeth shook her head in mock seriousness.

"That's my identical twin sitting over there," she said.

"And that's Enid!" called Todd suddenly, pointing toward the door.

Jessica squinted toward the front of the restaurant. "There's somebody with her, but I can't make out who it is."

Elizabeth turned around. "I don't believe it!" she exclaimed. "It's Hugh!"

"Have you got room for one more?" asked Enid, pulling Hugh along behind her. Her eyes were sparkling.

"What's going on here?" asked Elizabeth. "I thought you were never going to speak to Hugh again."

Enid blushed. "I know," she said, glancing shyly at Hugh. "But after the mess you got into because no one was really *talking* to anyone else, I decided I had to try and straighten things out."

Hugh put his arm around Enid. "So I know why Enid wouldn't return any of my calls."

"And I know why Hugh never showed up and that the girl in the bike shop was just a friend who was crying because she'd broken up with her boyfriend. And I know that Hugh really was following me around, trying to get me to talk to him."

"That's great," said Jessica, "we're all very happy for you. But do you think we could order now? I'm about to eat the red-pepper flakes."

Enid took the seat next to Elizabeth's. "And guess what else?" she asked her. "Hugh didn't really find my earring. He just said that so he could see me again!"

"But Enid," said Elizabeth, "Hugh couldn't have found your earring. You never lost one."

"That's right," gasped Enid. "I guess I forgot."

Elizabeth was still dreaming about her happy reunion with Todd when Jessica burst into her room Saturday morning.

"Liz, are you awake?" she asked in a stage whisper.

Elizabeth rubbed her eyes and then squinted at her sister. "I don't think so. I think I'm still dreaming. You're hardly ever up before me on a weekend."

Jessica plopped down on the bed next to Elizabeth. "I know, but I just couldn't sleep. I was thinking about how happy everyone is now—Enid's with Hugh again, and you're back with Todd, I'm with Sam—and then I got to thinking about how the only thing that could make me happier would be getting a Jeep. . . ."

Elizabeth groaned and pulled the sheet over her head. "Oh, no! Not the Jeep again! Jessica, that's all you've been talking about for weeks!"

Jessica pulled the sheet away from Elizabeth's face. "Just listen, OK?"

Elizabeth grinned. "Well, after you saved my reputation, my romance, and my friendship, I guess I owe you that much. Shoot."

"So, I got to thinking about all the places we could go with our Jeep. You know, without having to worry about breaking down. Places like Los Angeles. And thinking about Los Angeles made me think about the article I read about how *The Young and the Beautiful* might be looking for twins—"

"Whoa!" Elizabeth sat up and pushed her hair out of her eyes.

"I thought you said you owe me the courtesy of listening to me. Remember?"

"All right. I'll listen, but I don't promise anything."

Jessica beamed. "OK. So *if*, just *if*, the show really is looking for twins and we're the twins they're looking for, a Jeep would be the coolest way to travel. Right?"

Elizabeth shook her head and laughed. "Maybe it's because I just woke up, but I'm not sure I detect any logic in that argument." She playfully punched her sister's arm. "But, hey, I'll give you the benefit of the doubt. Yes, a Jeep would be the coolest mode of transportation. Satisfied?"

"Not yet." Jessica stood up and placed her hands on her hips. "I won't be satisfied until I'm sitting behind the wheel of a four-wheel-drive vehicle—cruising to Los Angeles to meet with my director!"

Will Jessica and Elizabeth become soap opera stars? Find out in Sweet Valley High #85, **SOAP STAR.**